Turkey Basted to Death

Turkey Basted to Death

Jodi Rath

Published by MYS ED LLC

PO Box 349

Carroll, OH 43112

First Printing, November 15, 2019

Copyright © Jodi Rath, 2019

All Rights Reserved

This is a work of fiction. Names, characters, places, and incidents either are the product of the author's imagination or are used fictitiously, and any resemblance to actual persons, living or dead, business establishments, events or locales is entirely coincidental.

The publisher does not have any control over and does not assume any responsibility for author or third-party websites or their content.

The scanning, uploading, and distribution of this book via the internet or any other means without the permission of the publisher are illegal and punishable by law. Please purchase only authorized electronic editions and do not participate in or encourage electronic piracy of copyrighted materials. Your support of the author's rights is appreciated.

https://www.jodirath.com

Note from the Publisher: The recipes contained in this book are to be followed exactly as written. Be aware that oven temperatures vary. The publisher and author are not responsible for your specific health or allergy needs that may require medical supervision. The publisher and author are not responsible for any adverse reactions to the recipes contained in this book or series.

Cover Design by Karen Phillips at Phillips Covers
www.PhillipsCovers.com

Edited by Rebecca Grubb at Sterling Words
www.sterlingwords.com

Formatted by Meredith Bond at Anessa Books
http://anessabooks.com

Leavensport, Ohio

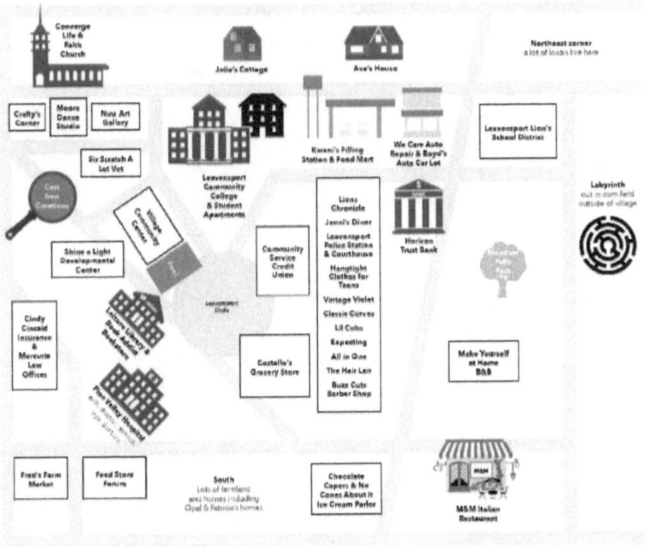

*Why can family push our buttons so easily?
They installed them! ~Jodi Rath*

The Leavensport Crew

Jolie Tucker—Co-owner of Cast Iron Creations, born in the village, best friend of Ava, granddaughter of Opal, daughter of Patty.

Ava Martinez—Co-owner of Cast Iron Creations, born in the village, best friend of Jolie, girlfriend of Delilah, sister of Lolly, daughter of Sophia and Thiago.

Keith—Ex-boyfriend of Jolie, born in the village, best friend of Teddy.

Detective Mick Meiser—Love interest of Jolie, from Tri-City, transferred career to Leavensport.

Chief Teddy Tobias—Police chief of Leavensport and born in the village, best friend of Keith.

Lydia—Jolie's frenemy, dating Bradley, village nurse, best friend of Betsy, born in the village.

Betsy—Owns Chocolate Capers, best friend of Lydia, born in the village.

Delilah—Sister of Bradley, village artist, girlfriend of Ava.

Bradley—Brother of Delilah, village journalist, dating Lydia.

Grandma Opal—Jolie's grandma, housewife who helped Jolie and Ava start Cast Iron Creations with her cast-iron skillet recipes.

Aunt Fern—Jolie's wacky, unpredictable aunt, sister to Patty, man-hungry.

Patty—Jolie's mom.

Uncle Wylie—Jolie's uncle.

Mirabelle and Spy—Hostess at Cast Iron Creations. Spy is her seeing-eye dog.

Carlos—Cook at Cast Iron Creations.

Mayor Nalini—Mayor of Leavensport

Mayor Cardinal—Mayor of Tri-City

Nestle—Unscrupulous political associate of Mayor Cardinal

Thiago Martinez—Ava's dad

Sophia Martinez—Ava's mom

Theo—Lolly's husband

Lolly—Ava's sister.

Acknowledgements

I am extremely grateful to work with such a terrific team to help make my series shine: Karen Phillips does incredible work on the covers (not to mention she puts up with my endless tweaks), Merry Bond's company does a fantastic job formatting all files of the books, and Rebecca Grubb from Sterling Words has gone above and beyond in helping to polish and edit the drafts from the big crapola first draft to the shiny and sparkly final draft that you all get to enjoy!

My family is all amazing. They provide me with never-ending encouragement and support and help me stay grounded and sane. My hubby Mike accepts me for all my successes and failures and loves me unconditionally—even when I'm freaking out and pulling out my already wild curls on deadline to finish these books. My nine fur babies are always around to jump on my keyboard, paw at me to stop and remember to love on them. They are also my inspiration: they show up on the covers and storyline of each book! My mom, my grandma, Mike Miller, my Uncle Willie and Aunt Patty, Kacy, Kyle, Sheila, Sherry, Tink, Aunt Ellen, Uncle Ernie, Grandpa, and my hubby's family Steve, Linda, Dottie, Linda, Bruce, Kellie, Justin, Kate, Joe, Heather, Bill, Bella, Harrison, and Adam all show up in one form or another in my series. They all have had a huge impact on my life in so many wonderful ways! Yes, there is dysfunction—what family doesn't have it? But they are all my rock and the foundation on which I stand—although no, I will not share any percentage of what I make with any of you! LOL!

All of my bestie girlfriends: Michelle, Rachel, Mary Ann, Leigh, Rebecca, Jancy, Amy, Cam, Stacy, Kim, Dr. Libby, and Janet all show up in one way or another in the book too! You all keep me laughing and accept me as I am—which we all know is a bit cray-cray!

Thanks to all my beta readers: Michele Wicker, Steve and Linda Rath, Rebecca Grubb, Susanna Grubb, Mary Ann Ware, and Rosie Walton.

The Guppies have all been my rock in helping me grow as a writer for years now.

Lastly, to all the readers—I don't have the words to describe what it means to me that you all follow me and write kind emails and messages and hang with me on social media and in my monthly newsletter. I would never have imagined a better audience for this series than all of you! The cozy community is truly an amazing place to be! Thank you all!

Love and Light!

Jodi

Chapter One

Monday, 11/25/19

Therapy journal prompt #1: Why am I going to therapy, and what do I hope to accomplish?

Honestly, I'm not enjoying therapy at all. I don't know why I thought it was supposed to be enjoyable. Tabitha is nice enough, but it's so weird discussing the darkest corners of my life with a complete stranger. Not to mention, I try NOT to think about those things—but Tabitha wants me to dredge it all up. I might tell her I'm quitting. I kind of don't think it's helpful to rehash the past. I can't understand how unburying past trauma can help me have a happier future. It's definitely not helping me have a happier now.

Ugh, and Thanksgiving is this Thursday. For reals? I'm so not in the holiday mood. Since Keith finished the police academy and works for Teddy, it seems like his life is one big ball of happiness. I can feel him trying to nudge us back into dating like we did in high school—it's so rough because I consider him an amazing friend. We grew up together, dated, then worked through the hurt I put him through to become friends again. He was the one who was honest with me about Meiser—or whatever his real name is—last summer. I need his friendship, but I don't know how to make that clear to him without hurting him again.

Speaking of Meiser, I HATE that when I see him, I still have tingles rush up and down my body. My stupid hoo-hah needs to get itself under control—and so does my heart. Logically, I know I can't be with a man who built the foundation of our relationship on lies. This is exactly what my bio father did with me from the time I was a toddler into my early teen years. Tabitha says those are the years when humans develop social and familial norms from observing the behaviors and environments around them. No wonder half the time I can't stand men and can't make a relationship work for the life of me! Sometimes I think Ava has it all figured out. Maybe if I was into women, I could make a relationship work? Maybe not? Trust. I have so few people I trust. I don't know how to change that.

Well, I guess for now, I'll continue avoiding Mick. Maybe quitting the therapy thing isn't such a great idea. At least this is one therapeutic homework assignment that's done. Time for cuddles in bed with the kitties, then sleep! Testing out more turkey Dutch cast-iron recipes in the morning.

The times are for sure a-changing. This time last year, I actually thought I was ready to *maybe* try dating again. I jumped on that topsy-turvy carnival ride called love—and I feel like I was at the top of the ride and fell off flat on my face. That's where I am now. Eating pavement.

"Aren't you supposed to be picking up your family at the airport now?" I asked Ava.

"They aren't getting in until later tonight. Papa wanted to finish up some last-minute work so he could enjoy the holiday," Ava said while testing out the fifth turkey recipe we had tried that week.

It's Thanksgiving this Thursday, and with Ava's family coming back to Leavensport, we decided to rent out the Community Center, and the majority of the village is having Thanksgiving dinner together. All of the restaurants in town are contributing to the dinner, and many of the villagers are making lots of food–like a potluck. I'd been testing out multiple turkey recipes for the big day. We were doing taste tests at the restaurant so the villagers could choose their favorites and then donating the remainder of the turkeys to the homeless shelter in Tri-City. So far, the Cajun turkey was a big hit as well as the smokehouse turkey and the honey turkey with lemon and sage.

"Is your therapist going to be at the Thanksgiving gathering?" Ava asked.

"I don't know. Why?" I asked sharply, tapping my foot in annoyance.

"Isn't that a conflict of interest? The two of you can't have dinner together, can you?" Ava scowled at my tone and took two steps back.

If only I could have seen my face at that moment. "She is my counselor, not my parole officer."

"Yeah, I know that. I'm just asking if it's a conflict of interest. Geesh!" Ava's voice shot up three octaves.

"You and my family know I'm seeing her. It's not a secret, but I'm not posting it on social media or anything. Everything I say is confidential. It's not like she will sit at the table and blab everything I've told her."

Ava's glare made me realize that my hands were on my hips, and I must have been giving her a look, not to mention I had used the "duh" tone with her. She was not happy with me at the moment.

"You know what, forget it!" Ava harrumphed. "I hope she does you some good. Your moods have been all over the place lately."

Flinching, I reached out and lightly touched her arm. "I'm sorry. I know I have been kind of...emotionally erratic. Honestly, I don't know if she will be there or not. If she is, I doubt I will talk to her much. She's nice enough, but we're not friends. Also, it is awkward living in a small village and seeing her all over the place. Truthfully, we tend to avoid each other in public. Which makes it weird sometimes."

"I can understand that."

"Are you excited to finally see your family?" I changed the topic.

"I'm nervous," Ava said. "We've never been away from each other for this long. What if they've changed a lot or if I've changed a lot? My mom is still doing that manipulative dance, being passive-aggressive about me deciding not to move with them."

"Don't worry. They'll be thrilled to see you!" I hoped I was right. The Martinez family had high expectations of their children. I remember when Ava told her mom she wanted to start the restaurant with me. Sophia wanted a spreadsheet of all projected expenses and profits and how much salary we planned to take in during the first year. We were five.

"Uh, Miss Jolie, you will want to come to front?"

Our cook Carlos popped his head into the kitchen. Ava followed me out.

"Hello, Mayor Nalini," I greeted him. "How can we help you?"

"Hi, ladies. Any new thoughts on the Thanksgiving gathering?" He rubbed the back of his neck and seemed to be having difficulty meeting my gaze.

Ava and I raised our eyebrows at each other. "Nope, just been testing out different recipes for turkeys. We've been working on the menu and did taste tests all last week."

"Okay, that's great. And Ava, excited to see your family?" the mayor asked.

"Sure, it will be good to see them again." She fumbled with her hands.

"Is there a problem?" I asked.

"What? Problem? No—of course not." The mayor shifted. "Actually, Ava, wouldn't you rather have a nice private dinner seeing that you and your family haven't had time together for a while?"

"Nooo." Ava drug out the word. "They can't stay long, and this will make it easier for them to be able to see everyone in town all at once. We will have time to visit with just our family for a little while before they leave."

"What is going on, Mayor?" I asked. Mayor Nalini was the one who was dead set on this big community holiday gathering to begin with. He came and pleaded with us in October to take on the majority of the catering for the event. Now he was behaving oddly.

"I just got off the phone with Mayor Cardinal in Tri-City," he began.

Oh no, I felt my heart sink into my chest. Whatever he was about to say could not be good news.

Chapter Two

"So, what does the good Mayor Cardinal of Tri-City have up his sleeve this time?" I narrowed my eyes.

"I've never known you to be so cynical, Jolie." Mayor Nalini looked concerned.

"Well, a lot can change when we grow up, sir. I learned a little about how politics works this last summer—politics can make a cynic out of the best of us," I said. Ava nodded in agreement.

Last summer, there was a buzz about urban sprawl in our little village. A lot of the land had been bought, and there was talk about many businesses and possible low-income apartments being built. Development was creeping out of Tri-City and down the highway. It was easy to see how someday the village might be absorbed by the larger metropolis. There were some crooked developments that had never been fully revealed— but Nestle, a man many thought was associated with Mayor Cardinal, ended up being taken to jail. He wasn't convicted of anything, though. For now, the sale of some of the land in question had been stalled. No one had started building anything, and there were no for-sale signs at this point. Things seemed to be at a standstill for the moment.

"So, Mister Mayor, lay it on us." Ava spoke through clenched teeth.

"It seems that Mayor Cardinal believes I owe him a favor after losing the opportunity to purchase some of our land earlier in the year." He paused to clear his throat, eyeballing me. "Like you said, Jolie."

"MM-HMM..." I nodded slowly, waiting for whatever was next.

"Mayor Cardinal is in a bit of a jam. He has a teen advocate who has been pressuring him into allowing her to use one of the city facilities to host a holiday event for the inner-city youth. The mayor has other plans. This young lady is rather persistent. So, he'd like me to repay the favor by opening up Leavensport Community Center for the event for the inner-city teens this Thursday." The mayor pressed his lips together and rubbed his jawline, waiting for our response.

"Oh, you have got to be kidding me!" Ava yelled. "NO WAY!"

"When did he contact you?" I asked.

"This morning."

"I understand the whole you-scratch-my-back-I'll-scratch-yours political angle, but you're just going to stand for this bullying?" I spat out—a little like a bully myself.

"Hey, I need to stay on his good side. In the coming years, our village will become more dependent on the folks in the city," the mayor said.

"What are you talking about?" I asked, hands on hips. I was getting tired of what felt like a cat-and-mouse game with the politicians. Nothing had been completely resolved from last summer, when our fine mayor had acknowledged the potential of urban sprawl.

"Just figure it out, Jolie," he said firmly. "Either find a way to share the day with the teens or move the holiday to another day or place." The mayor looked exhausted.

"We can't find another place on this short of notice and let everyone know!" Ava exclaimed.

"The community center is big enough to hold the villagers attending and some teenagers," the mayor replied.

"Who is the teen advocate?" I asked.

The mayor took out his phone and began swiping. "A Pria Stephens," he said, holding up a text message. Mayor Nalini was a nice-looking older man with slicked-back gray hair and a dark complexion. He had emigrated from India to Leavensport as a child and had lost his wife several years ago after twenty-five years of marriage. My Aunt Fern did a lot of flirting with him—but she was known to flirt with most of the older gentlemen around the village.

"Do you know how I can get in contact with her?"

"Call the mayor's office?"

"As always, you're a huge help," Ava huffed and spun around, stomping off.

"What's with her? Does she hate teenagers or something?" Mayor Nalini rolled his eyes.

"She's freaked out about her family showing up, and this is a bit of a surprise to us all," I replied. "I mean, you're asking us to make more food with little to no notice for a bunch of people we don't even know. Have you talked to others in the village? Some of them will not be thrilled with this news."

"No, I don't know that there is time to call a meeting, and even if we did, I'm not sure how many would show up on such short notice," Mayor Nalini said.

"*Thanks*, Mayor Nalini," I snapped. "I'll see what I can figure out. Now you know how *we* feel being given this task with no notice—you can't even let your constituents know what is happening on the holiday event *you* created!" I knew my Aunt Fern would have my head if she found out I sassed the mayor.

Walking back to the kitchen, I was greeted by the smell of garlic, onion, and melting cheddar cheese— my mouth instantly began to water. Carlos, our cook, was prepping for the lunch rush, whipping up shredded pot roast and au gratin potatoes.

"Hey Carlos, do you recognize the name Pria Stephens?" I asked, knowing he grew up in Tri-City and that he had a rough start in life. Carlos had shared much of his childhood with me during his interview. His parents were from Mexico and came to America undocumented to escape some horrific abuses from the mafia. Carlos was born on the south side of Tri-City. His mom and dad had worked three or more jobs each to make enough to afford a roof over their heads and food on the table. He had spent most of his childhood at the city's YMCA and his teen years at the community activism center. Carlos always wore T-shirts with cartoon characters like Scobby-Doo or the Roadrunner on them. He told me his mom and dad always spoke Spanish when he was growing up, so that was the language he learned at home. When started school, he struggled with English, and American cartoons helped him pick it up. He even had an Oscar the Grouch T-shirt.

"I think she took the place of the last teen counselor after I stopped hanging out at the center."

"Mayor Nalini called her a teen advocate, not a counselor," I said, making sure I contacted the right person.

"Same thing, Miss Jolie. The younger counselors like to call themselves advocates to make the teens feel more comfortable."

I could understand that. I wish Tabitha would call herself my advocate and not my therapist. I never stopped to think about how much the change of a word can matter.

"Do you know how I can get in contact with that department—like now?"

"Can you take over here for a minute, and I'll go make a few calls?" Carlos asked.

"Sure thing," I said, taking over slicing some potatoes. Our lunch special of the day featured our cast-iron spin on potatoes au gratin as a side dish for the shredded pot roast.

Ava, who typically did nothing in the kitchen except gossip, came barreling out of the office and snatched a pair of nitrile gloves, popped them on, grabbed the nearest potato, and began chopping in a fury.

"Whoa! Stop!" I yelled, hand in the air.

"What?" she snapped.

"We are *slicing* these, not massacring them, and...since when do you help out in the kitchen?"

"Since I need to use a weapon!" Ava brandished the large chef knife rather maniacally.

"Mmmkay..." I said, backing down. "Just slice, please."

She continued hacking, ignoring my pleas. "I am so sick of the politics around here lately. I haven't seen my parents in a year, and because some pompous city mayor wants to puff his chest out, our holiday has to be ruined."

I remembered why we kept Ava out of the kitchen. She was like a bull in a china shop. Hopefully, I could find a way to calm her down and get her back up front before she destroyed any more potatoes.

"Just don't worry," I said. "I'll see what I can do. Please put the knife down and go up and check on Mirabelle and Spy for me." That would put Ava in a better mood. Mirabelle was our "hostess with the mostess," as Aunt Fern liked to call her. She was a woman with Down Syndrome and had sight issues, so she sat on a stool at the front of the shop with her seeing-eye dog, Spy, and greeted people as they came and went.

Ava reluctantly put the knife down and headed up front. Then she stopped for a moment, turned back to me and said, "You know I'm not a horrible person, right?"

"Of course, I know that! Why would you ask such a thing?"

"I just realized that I'm pouting about some kids with rough lives intruding on my family's holiday." She shook her long, thick locks.

I took a moment to contemplate what she had said. "We react in the moment. We're human," I said finally.

"Yeah...okay." Ava seemed lost in thought.

I wasn't used to seeing her so serious. I put some lemon juice on the potato that Ava had just destroyed and stored it in the fridge, figuring I'd find a way to use it even if it meant having it for lunch one day. I hated to waste food.

Carlos came back in from the alley and grabbed a sheet of paper and a pen from the office and wrote down some phone numbers. He had on a Sylvester and Tweety T-shirt today.

"Here you go, Miss Jolie. I called some old contacts and got this information for you. The first number is Pria's direct cell number. If you can't reach her, then call the second number, and she will get the message," Carlos smiled, swapping places with me.

"You're the best, Carlos!"

I tried Pria's cell phone first. It rang and went to voicemail.

It's Pria! Why are you calling me? Get with the times—text!

I opted to be old-fashioned. I left a pleasant message that ended with me asking her to call me back ASAP.

Next, I tried the second number and got an answer before the end of the first ring. "Yo!"

"Um, hello. Pria?"

I heard what sounded like loud chomping. "Nah, this isn't Pria. She be chillaxin at the rec center with the others."

"Do you know how I can reach her there?"

A series of giggles, more loud chomping, and a disconnect.

Well, it looked like I was heading up to the Tri-City Rec Center.

Walking into the rec center, I looked around, trying to figure out who Pria could be. Everyone in this place looked like a teenager. I heard some yelling in the gym and walked through the auditorium doors seeing a line of teens against the wall with one pony-tailed blonde holding a red rubber ball, aiming at one of the teens. Squeals of laughter rang out, echoing from the gym.

Taking a step inside, I looked across the gym and saw a young woman with coal-black, short, spiky hair, shouting encouragement as a young man attempted to climb a rope to ring a bell at the top.

"You got this, Stella!" she yelled, clapping her hands as the young man stopped mid-rope. "This is where you determine who you are! Do you stop and drop or swallow the pain and keep climbing? Only you can decide that!"

The young man looked down with large dark eyes, seeming to question his strength, then looked up, measuring the distance.

I was guessing one reason he would be struggling is that he seemed to have baggy sweats on with a too-large T-shirt. He had long hair pulled up in a man-bun.

"Half-way there, girl! You got this! Dig deep!"

Girl?

"Think of everything you've been through, a few more pulls—dig deep!"

I felt myself internally rooting for this person. *You got this! Dig deep! Just a few more pulls of your body weight to ring that bell! Draw on your inner strength! Please—you got it, DO IT!*

It's like I mentally encouraged the kid. A look of determination and fight entered the teen's eyes, taking a big breath, the kid grunted obnoxiously and pulled hard. BOOM! One more pull and the teenager had it. A battle cry came as the youth jerked hard and Stella pulled her body up, reaching for the bell and hitting it hard. Then, the kid slid carefully but quickly down the rope. The group on the other side of the gym stopped their game of dodge ball and came running and yelling in glee.

"Steeellllaaaaaaa!!!!" someone screamed like Brando in *A Streetcar Named Desire*. "You did it, GIRLLLLL!"

"Go, girlfriend, GO!"

The girl started crying tears of joy as the spiky-haired lady grabbed her and hugged her.

A boy looked over at me. "Hey, who are you?"

Suddenly, all eyes turned to me, and I felt like an intruder. Oddly enough, I became keenly aware of the smell of sweat and stinky socks in that moment of awkwardness.

The spiky-haired lady walked over, "I'm sorry, but we are on the schedule for the rec center today."

"I don't mean to intrude, but do you know a Pria Stephens?"

"Who wants to know?" the lady asked from behind a smile that didn't quite reach her eyes.

"I'm Jolie Tucker. I'm from Leavensport, and it's my understanding Miss Stephens is using our community center for Thanksgiving this Thursday? I tried calling two numbers and found out she may be here."

"Oh. Yeah, I'm Pria," she said, reaching out a hand, and I saw her smile grow sincere.

"It's nice to meet you." I shook her hand. "Do you have a few minutes to talk, or should I come back later?"

"Hey, Shelly, can you take over for a few? I'm going to run out for a bit," she yelled over to someone who looked to be, at best, a teenager.

The lady nodded in confirmation, and I followed Pria out of the gym.

"Want a piece of blueberry pie?" Pria asked over her shoulder.

"Sure," I said. *Who wouldn't?*

"Have you had Peggy's Pies before?"

"Nope, can't say that I have."

"Peggy's cool. She owns the pie shop and has a purse boutique that is connected to it. You can walk up to the register with a pie in one hand and a purse in the other."

"Pies and purses? Um, I'm in!" I exclaimed.

Pria grinned. "Right?"

We were seated, and I took her suggestion and ordered the blueberry pie. I got hot tea, and she got coffee, which smelled delicious. I love the smell of coffee, but I've never been able to drink it. It gives me a stomachache. I looked around the restaurant—even though it was located in the city, it had a small-town diner feel with large red booths, a black-and-white checkered tile floor, an old-style jukebox in the corner, and a counter with short, red Naugahyde stools. I had half-expected Peggy to come out on roller skates, wearing a ponytail, popping pink bubblegum while she took our order.

"So, you're upset that we're using your community center too?" Pria asked bluntly.

Nervously, I went to put my fork down and knocked my huge tote over, and everything spilled out of it. Pria was nice enough to bend over and help. "Sorry," I muttered. "I'm a bit of a klutz."

Pria laughed. "Me too!" She reached to grab a loose piece of paper that flew to the next table. She flinched and averted her eyes, then looked awkward as she handed it to me.

I had absentmindedly written, "I HATE THERAPY JOURNALING!" and decorated the paper with swirls and frowny faces, even skull and crossbones in the corner. "Sorry, I couldn't help but notice what it said. I swear I wasn't trying to be nosey."

I giggled. "What? You mean you couldn't control your eyeballs from seeing the huge black Sharpie bubble letters?"

Pria's body had been tense, but I saw her let out a deep breath and laugh with me.

"I did the whole journaling, therapy thing too. I get it. I hated it so much," she said.

"You did? I feel like no one else does this but me. I forget others do therapy all the time. As you can see, I'm not subtle about my feelings on it."

"It's not something most people announce, and I'm not sure I've met anyone who loves it."

"True, I keep teetering back and forth on the idea of stopping, but every time I'm positive I should stop either something helps me or something crazy happens that makes me realize I need it," I said, folding the paper and shoving it back in my purse.

"I think that's a very normal, human thing to do."

"Wow, you really did go through it—you sound just like a therapist!" I said.

"Well, I am a teen counselor, so, I guess it's close enough."

"No offense, but you look like a teenager yourself," I said.

"Hey, thanks, when I was a teen, you would have thought I looked a decade older. That's why I had to do therapy and why I do what I do now. I'm a lesbian, and when I came out, my parents kicked me out. I went to three cities before I had an opportunity to get myself out of the street life."

"Three cities?" I asked. That seemed like a strange thing to say.

"Yeah, being young, I needed money. In the first city I went to, Bucklin, I refused to do—well, you know, the thing a lot of girls have to do on the streets for money—so, I ended up finding a homeless shelter where I could get a place to sleep and food. The politicians wanted to gentrify the town–build condos, clubs, and small businesses. So, the police worked with the politicians to kick us all out. There were other parts of the city I could have gone to, but I moved to a new city with a friend I had made."

"Wow, sometimes I feel so sheltered. I grew up in a small village where we all know each other. Last year, we had this scare of urban sprawl. I'd never heard of it before. It feels wrong to even say it like that—we had a 'scare.'" I said.

"I mean, I get it. It's a tough thing. People that have money want nice things. People in poverty don't have a lot of power. You live in a beautiful area. You want to protect that. I'm not sure there is a good solution," Pria said.

I hated how much I loved this lady. She was so cool and smart!

"Yeah, the older I get, the more I realize how much I don't know. I always thought the older I got, the wiser I would get. It seems to be the opposite. So, how'd you end up here? You said three cities, right?"

"Oh, yeah. In the second city, my friend I went with stayed with a guy named Smalls—I don't know what his real name is..." Pria stared off into the distance as though reliving the past.

I couldn't help thinking *I know the feeling.*

"Anyway, he had me steal for him, but he took care of us otherwise. I'm not proud of that time in my life. Long story short, Smalls fell for me, but I like the ladies—so when he made a pass, I turned him down. He wasn't a great guy. I got away, and since I was used to stealing, I stole some money and ended up here in Tri-City."

"Wow, do you mind me asking how old you are now?"

"I'll be twenty-six in December," she said, "I came here and realized I needed to find a way out of the street life. One day I walked into the Tri-City Public Library and asked the librarians for help. They saved my life. Like, literally saved my life. They let me couch surf when I didn't have shelter. I went there daily and signed up for an online school and got my diploma. They showed me how to apply for college and grants and financial aid. I got my bachelor's, and I'm currently working on my master's at the same time I'm working for the city to help the inner-city teens." She grinned proudly.

"Wow, you are like a superhero!" When I heard stories like hers, it made my own problems feel microscopic. I wondered why I struggled so much.

Pria laughed out loud, "I wish! I love where I'm at in life now. Actually, I ended up falling for one of those librarians. Her name is Stef."

"What a story! I'm so happy you are in a better place. Your story has to help those kids you work with."

"I hope so. Unfortunately, I am back at fighting the politicians over gentrification again. The mayor is sick of me—it's why we got pushed on you, I suppose."

"Yeah, I was coming here to see if you'd be willing to change your date," I said, feeling like a turd.

"I get it. I wanted the kids to get a holiday *on* a holiday, and to have a warm place with good food. They never get that. You know that girl Stella that climbed the rope?"

"She's a girl? I thought she looked more like a boy," I said curiously. "I'm sorry, that was probably a horrid thing to say. I swear I'm not one of those people who judges. I just don't always know how to react or what's the right thing to say. Plus, I get confused. Please don't hold it against me."

"That's normal, too, Jolie. And don't feel you have to apologize. It can be confusing. I believe it's all in the intention behind the comments. It's obvious you're not judging and that you are curious. Stella's in the process of transitioning: she's about two weeks into taking hormones right now. She will do some surgeries later. She reminds me of me. She was not accepted for who she is by her family, so she ran away. She's been struggling lately. I realized that finding ways to have the kids overcome things like climbing a rope when they find that difficult can help with what's going on internally with them."

"And here I thought my past was traumatic. So many people have had it so much worse."

"Don't say that! Your issues are still very real to you. Yes, everyone has different demons they carry around with them. We could compare them, but we shouldn't. Your issues should not be diminished because you hear other peoples' stories. Each of us has our weight to carry, and things to figure out."

"You really will be a wonderful therapist," I said, grinning. "How many people do you have coming on Thursday?"

"Well, I'd have some staff there to help keep the teens under control. So, I'd say no more than fifteen to twenty max." Pria lit up. "Wait, are you actually thinking about letting us use the community center on Thanksgiving Day?"

"Are you opposed to sharing the community center with our village? It is huge, and we can easily fit another twenty or thirty. Not everyone in the village will be there."

"You wouldn't mind sharing?"

"Not at all, and my best friend, Ava, and I co-own Cast Iron Creations. We and other restaurants and bakeries around the village are catering. So, if you can get me a headcount, we'll take care of the food, and you just bring yourselves."

Pria's eyes filled with tears. "I'm used to having to fight for everything. I've been lobbying for city council to use the money they want to use for condos and instead use it for a homeless shelter, and a community hall where we can give classes and help people get jobs and housing. It's been a battle."

"Well, this is one fight you don't have to have. We'll see you on Thursday around two in the afternoon. Okay?" I stood, grabbing my tote bag, and reached out my hand to shake hers.

Pria leapt up and grabbed me, hugging me tightly. I returned the squeeze.

Chapter Three

It was Thanksgiving Day. I wasn't feeling it at all. I hoped the turkeys I made turned out okay. I know this is weird, but I truly believe that the mood and energy of the cook makes a big difference in how the food turns out. At least Carlos was helping me. It's one of many reasons why I hired him. He was always in a good mood, and always so polite. Maybe he put some good juju vibes into the meal—hopefully, he had enough for both of us.

I went to the community center super early to help finish up the meals and decorate. Although most of the village was okay with the teens coming today, some of the community were NOT happy about the uninvited guests. I hoped we would still have a good turnout. I didn't have the energy to deal with any drama.

Of course, as soon as I had that thought, Ava came bursting through the doors in a panic.

"I *knew* I shouldn't have made a big deal out of my family coming. I mean, what was I thinking?" Ava was wearing an oversized sweatshirt with a cartoon lion talking to a cartoon turkey on it. The lion said, "You are looking yummy today, and I'm not Li-ON to you!"

"Ava, I'm so tired. I've been here for hours, and I'm not thrilled about the holidays."

"You're not thrilled? *You're* not thrilled?" She crossed her arms over the comical sweatshirt.

"No, you're right," I said with a fake chipper tone, "I am actually SUPER EXCITED. Can't you tell from my face?"

"You know better than anyone how dysfunctional families work. Why wouldn't you warn me not to invite my family?" Ava looked ready for battle with hands on hips and head cocked to one side.

"I'm sorry—I should tell you not to invite your family to Thanksgiving?" I snapped. I had no patience left. "How is any of this my fault? Wait, I don't even know what is or isn't my fault!" I went from anger to the edge of tears. "What is going on?" I wailed. *Oh, my word! No one had even showed up yet and I was already exhausted and ready to cry.*

"First off, their flight was late," Ava began. "You know how Papa gets when things don't run on time. So, he's grumpy when he walks up to me."

Yes, Thiago Martinez was extremely precise in how his schedule should go. His wife, Sophia, spoiled him in a lot of ways. She was as obsessive about routine and schedules as he was. It was always amazing to me that Ava didn't drive them insane over the years. She was anything but a routine-oriented, on-time person. She even drove disorganized me batty at times.

"Then, my mama walked right in front of Papa, grabbed my arm, and pulled me aside, and whispered, 'Theo cheated on your sister Lolly! Do not say anything!' And, here come Theo and Lolly. I mean, I don't even know how to digest any of this!" Ava looked like she was about to hyperventilate.

"Take a few breaths. Here, have a cup of coffee," I said, pouring a big mugful. "It's decaf."

"Good, I don't need anything else getting my heart rate up right now."

"Wow, I can't believe Theo cheated on Lolly. I would think it would be the other way around," I said, reaching for my big purple mug that had a wide-eyed black cat and the word "Meoweinated" on the side. It was perfect for sipping my favorite pumpkin tea.

"Why would you say that?" Ava glared at me.

"Sorry, I just meant your sister is so beautiful, and Theo is so...pocket-protector-like. *Why* would he want to cheat on your sister?" I asked incredulously.

"I don't know. But I must have been glaring at him in the rear-view mirror on the way to my house," Ava snorted.

"Why do you say that?"

"Because my mom was sitting behind me and she reached and grabbed my earlobe and about pulled it off my head." Ava rubbed her ear.

Ah, I remember upsetting Miss Sophia, and those ear grabs. When we were kids and made her really angry, she'd grab each of our earlobes and pull down, so our bodies were bent over, then she'd drag us into another room. It was not pleasant. I learned to behave around her. Ava—not so much.

"Great, another reason today will suck. Between *my* wacko family, *your* family's issues, half the village angry over the teens from Tri-City coming, and my foul mood—well, I can't imagine it can get any worse," I sighed.

A few hours later, I had finished up prep and ran back to the bathroom. I rooted around in my tote until I found my pick, then tried to bring some order to my curls. Then, a touch of blush and lip gloss. If I was moody, I could at least try to be a half-way decent-looking moody person.

I pushed through the door and heard someone on the other side grunt, "Ow!"

"Oh man, I'm sorry!" I stopped dead in my tracks. It was Meiser–or Milano, I should say.

"Hey, slugger," he said, trying to be nonchalant.

Detective Mick Meiser showed up in our village a little over a year ago. My life had been a roller coaster ride since. I was cautious at first, but with time he grew on me. I found myself doing something I hadn't done in more than a decade— trusting a man again. The last time I completely trusted a man was when my stepdad was alive. He died of prostate cancer when I was younger. However, Meiser followed in the footsteps of the majority of men in my life, most notably my *biological* father. Like them, he lied to me and made me feel like a fool.

"Oh, hey, um Meiser or...Milano." My voice cracked with pain and anger. "I'm not sure what to call you anymore."

Meiser blew out a breath and put his hands in his pockets. He looked at the ground, "How many times are you going to make me go through this, Jolie? I told you I legally changed my name to Mick Meiser. I'm still Meiser to you, and always will be."

"Right, well, I need to go check on the Cajun turkey. See you later, Mick."

I turned to walk away, and he grabbed my hand and spun me around. I *hated* that his touch still sent shivers through my body. "Please don't." I pulled my arm away.

"I'm sorry. I will continue to say it as long as you need me to say it. I will be saying it ten years from now if need be. I will say it until you forgive me, Jolie."

"Look, I told you, I'm not ready right now. I need time. I'm working through things."

"How much time? It's been close to six months. I miss you. I miss what we were starting."

"I know. Me too," I looked at the ground. "I've been doing therapy for the last two months. So, if you were serious about waiting, then wait. I can't tell you how long. And if you don't want to wait, then I get that. Do what you need to do, and I'll do what I need to do."

"I don't mean to be impatient. It's not a great holiday anyway. Some of my family was supposedly showing up today, but they canceled. I'm happy about it—I guess."

"You know why family can push your buttons, don't you?" I asked.

"Why?"

"Because they installed them."

"Hashtag truth," he grinned.

"Whoa, old man dropping the hashtag on me," I said, cackling and taking a step back, palms up as though disarmed by his coolness.

He did his hearty laugh that turns into a goofy sounding Scooby-Doo giggle when he chuckles too long. My cheeks started to hurt. I hadn't smiled that big in a while. The full impact of the situation hit me, and I felt tears well up.

"Gotta go," I said, rushing off. Phew, that was close. Note to self: journal about this for therapy. I don't want to slip back into trusting him only to be hurt again.

I walked into the kitchen and couldn't believe how much food we had. It looked like everyone in the village that attended had brought something. I'd made several different types of small turkey breasts in my Dutch cast iron pots. We had Cajun turkey, cranberry stuffed turkey, turkey breast roulade with apple raisin stuffing, and a maple glazed turkey roast. There were multiple types of potato dishes, vegetables, fruit, stuffing, casseroles, and so much more. Betsy, the owner of Chocolate Capers and one of my childhood friends, loaded us up on chocolate cream pies, multi-layered chocolate cakes, brownies, cookies, and cake pops for the kids that had adorable fall decorations on them like little turkeys, pumpkins, and cornucopias.

The smell of the food made my stomach growl, and it took me back to a memory of when Meiser and I were going to have dinner together. I met him at his house and surprised him by picking him up. He reached down and lightly brushed my cheek with his thumb while cupping my chin with his strong hand. It was only a second but staring into those sea-of-love eyes felt like an eternity as he leaned in closer...then my stupid stomach growled! But we laughed so hard we fell onto the floor—we were literally rolling on the floor laughing. Then, we began rolling around on the floor doing other things—

Right then, at an inopportune time, a girl walked in with a huge stack of pizzas in her hands. She looked very familiar to me, but I couldn't place from where.

"Hey Stella, long time no see," our part-time waitress from the restaurant, Magda, ran over to help Stella with the pizzas.

Wow, that was Stella from the rec center? At the gym, she had her hair pulled back, but today she had beautiful straight black hair cut in layers around her face, make-up done subtly with a black romper dress. She seemed very shy and reached out to hug Magda after unloading about eight pizza boxes on the counter.

"Yum, pizza!" I exclaimed.

Magda introduced us, "Oh, hey Jolie, this is my friend Stella. Stella, this is my boss, Jolie."

Stella reached out a hand and lightly shook mine. "I saw you the other day at the gym."

"Yeah, I saw you climb that rope. That was something else. I could not do that. I have no upper body strength at all."

"Oh, me neither. I'm sure you could do it if you put your mind to it," Stella said quietly. I had to lean in to hear her.

"How do you two know each other?" I asked.

"Magda works at the youth center as a volunteer sometimes. She was instrumental in helping me with my transition," Stella said.

Magda cleared her throat loudly. "Jolie, I'm transgender."

I hate to admit that my mind stopped momentarily in a bit of shock. "Okay, I didn't know that, but great!"

Magda had recently moved to the village when she started college and came in for lunch one day. She and Ava hit it off immediately, and it turned into her working for us part-time.

Magda grinned at me. My brain screeched to a halt. *Did I just say something dumb?*

"I'm sorry, was that stupid or insensitive to say?" I took a sharp breath in and rubbed my hands on my pants.

"Not at all. I wish everyone was so laid back about it."

"I see you every day and I had no idea. I mean, it doesn't make a difference, of course. But, if I ever accidentally say or do anything offensive, will you please tell me immediately?"

"You got it!" Magda grinned, putting an arm around me.

I relaxed and turned to the other girl. "Stella, you all didn't need to bring pizzas. I told Pria we'd take care of the food today."

"Oh, she wouldn't hear of it," replied Stella enthusiastically. "She used some of the youth center funds, and she put some of her own money in too. We get Ralph's pizza all the time. He gives us a discount. We didn't want to come empty-handed."

"I've heard Ralph's has the real-deal New York Pizza! This is Ralph's pizza?" I asked, lifting a lid and feeling drool run out of my mouth. I couldn't help myself, and rudely reached for a piece of pepperoni and cheese. I took a huge bite, grinning at the two girls with grease running down my chin. It melted in my mouth—there was a burst of parmesan and garlic explosion with a slight bit of heat from the spices in the pepperoni.

They both cracked up. Stella said, "I'm so happy I'm not the only one who steals food before it's time to eat!" She grabbed a piece, and so did Magda, and we all stuffed our faces.

Mid-chew, the door flew open and Ava and Grandma Opal thundered in. Grandma shoved her phone at me excitedly, squawking, "Here, Jolie, take a selfie of me!"

I almost spit partially chewed pizza out of my mouth.

"Huh?"

Magda choked on her pizza, and Stella smiled involuntarily. They both giggled and edged out of the kitchen, leaving us to grapple with whatever situation was in store for us.

"I told her you can't, by definition, take a *selfie* of *her*," Ava rolled her eyes. "It's literally in the name. *Self-eee!*"

"Yes, she can," Grandma Opal charged on heedlessly. "I want it close-up like those selfies. Here Jolie, get me close-up so people can see my new permed-do. That Bradley is out there taking pictures for the paper. He wanted to take one of me, but I told him I'd prefer to take my own picture and I'd send it to him. I don't trust that he'll get my best side."

"For it to be a selfie, you need to take it yourself. Like this," I said, holding the camera out and taking a picture of myself.

"I tried to explain it to her. I showed her, too," Ava said, shoulders drooping in defeat.

"Nevermind, I'm good to go, girls, thanks!" Grandma Opal trotted out the kitchen door.

Our heads snapped up, and our eyes followed her. "What is that crazy coot up to?" I wondered as we followed her into the auditorium.

"Patty, Fernie, I got them. Those two are the definition of gullible," Grandma Opal yelled across the hall, waving her phone in the air.

"What exactly do you have, Grandma?" I asked.

Grandma was making a beeline for the Martinezes and the Tuckers, who were eating and talking in a group. Ava and I followed her over.

"Opal, thank you. Could you please text both pictures to me?" Ava's mom, Sophia, asked.

"Sure thing," my grandma said, but not before stopping, holding the phone up in the air, tilting her head up with chin up and smiling her pearly whites to get her selfie. "There you go. I figured you'd like to have one of me too." Grandma winked at Sophia, and then went running toward Bradley to no doubt push her selfie onto him for the village paper.

"Why, what is going on?" Ava raised her voice.

"*Cuida tu tono*, Ava!" Mrs. Martinez barked. "I wanted a picture on my phone of my two girls who I never see any more so I can show you both off in Santo Domingo. I knew I wouldn't be able to get you two to take a picture for me, so Miss Opal took care of it for me."

I side-whispered to Ava, "what'd she say at first?"

"'*Watch your tone*,'" Ava whispered back, shaking her head.

I averted my eyes back to Sophia to see if she saw Ava shake her head in annoyance; I was afraid for my earlobe right now. Luckily, she didn't seem to notice.

Suddenly, our conversation was interrupted by several raised voices. We all abruptly turned our heads. Three teens were yelling at Pria while a fourth teen sat on a bench, looking humiliated.

"Calm down," Pria said quietly. "Take a few

breaths. We are in public, and we have been invited here. Show some respect and decency. I expect you all to apologize to Tink and mind your manners for the rest of our visit."

The three mumbled an insincere apology to the red-headed, freckled-faced boy that was sulking on the bench, and then they walked outside.

I walked over to check on Pria. "Are you okay?"

"I apologize, Jolie. Tink is new to our group, and some of the others aren't being as welcoming as I've taught them to be."

"Jolie? Jolie *Tucker*?" The boy looked at me in bewilderment, like he knew me.

"Yes, how do you know my last name?"

The boy blushed and backtracked. "Oh, I-uh-I heard some of the others talking about you from when you were at the gym."

"Well, it's nice to meet you–" I smiled at him, "Tink was it?"

"Yeah, my name is Ed Jr., but everyone's always called me Tink. Long story."

I nodded at him and turned to Pria.

"I wanted to thank you for bringing the pizza, but you didn't have to do that."

She grinned. "I heard you already enjoyed some."

"You like pizza too? It's my favorite food!" Tink stood up, bouncing from foot to foot with a gleam in his eyes.

"Yeah, mine too," I said.

"Tink, will you go out and ask them to come back in so we can all introduce ourselves and apologize for our rudeness, please?" Pria said.

Tink's smile shifted to a resentful grimace. "You shouldn't have made a scene here," he growled. "You could have ignored it or dealt with it later. I can take care of myself."

"Tink, we deal with things as they happen."

His shoulders tightened and his fists clenched.

"You're like every other adult!" His voice was getting louder. "You *mortified* me! I wish you'd disappear!" The conversation had escalated abruptly.

"Tink, don't start again," Pria said firmly. "Please do as I said, or there will be consequences for your actions."

"I wish you were dead," he muttered and stomped off.

I bit my lower lip and studied the floor in the awkward silence that followed.

"Teens," Pria slumped her shoulders. "They'll calm down once we feed them."

"Yes, food makes everything better," I agreed. "Hey, I'll be right back, okay?" I ran over to Ava.

"What's up with the brat pack?" Ava asked as I approached.

We both looked over toward Pria. She seemed lost in thought, then suddenly punched the wall in frustration. Ava and I gasped. As we watched, Pria put her hands over her face, took a deep breath, then stalked away. It was obvious she didn't think anyone noticed.

"Just teenage shenanigans." I said, feeling my mouth go dry from the scene I just witnessed, "Hey, can you run over to the restaurant and grab that new stainless-steel turkey baster I bought last week? I forgot Carlos told me this morning that the plastic one broke. We have to keep these turkeys juicy until dinnertime."

"Sure thing, be right back."

While Ava went to grab the turkey baster, Pria brought the teens back in and asked for everyone's attention. She had transitioned back into the cool and calm Pria. She introduced herself and shared little bits and pieces of her story that she had shared with me, explaining what she did and introducing several of the teens. She thanked the villagers for their kind-heartedness and apologized for the earlier scene—looking at the teens. Several of them looked apologetic and smiled with a little wave.

Even though several of the villagers were upset earlier in the week, after Pria gave her speech, the villagers mingled and mixed with the newcomers, introducing themselves and asking questions. I grabbed the appetizers and put them out at tables as others helped.

Ava came blasting in with a broken, sharp turkey baster.

"What happened? We just bought that!" I yelled, squeezing my eyes shut to gain control.

"Calm down! You are so cheap! It was like fifteen bucks, Jolie."

"That's expensive for a turkey baster! How on earth do you break a stainless-steel baster? It's the kitchen equivalent of *bullet-proof*!!"

Ava had a look of chagrin, then stuck her chin out. "I, uh, ran over it."

Only Ava could do this. I stood with arms out, waiting for an explanation.

"I saw someone—and I am pretty sure it was

Nestle—peeking in the window, so I yelled at him. I must have set the baster on the roof of my car. He jumped in a car, and I took off after him but lost him. The baster fell off the car. When I pulled back to pull in to park, I ran over it. See? It was an accident. Could have happened to anyone."

"Nestle? What on earth is he up to? He knows he's not wanted around here," I said, remembering all the sketchy things he did last summer, like trying to threaten Ava's girlfriend, Delilah, into selling her family's art shops.

Pria came over. "Hey, ladies, what's up?"

"Ava ran over my new turkey baster," I wailed.

"Let me take it in the back and see if I can fix it long enough to work for you today," Pria said.

"Do you think you can?" I pleaded.

"I've gotten pretty good at fixing things to save money. Be right back!"

"I love her! She's great," I said.

"Yeah, she's super cool!" Ava said. I glanced over Ava's shoulder out of the full-length windows in front of the building and stopped short. Was that Meiser? He was talking to a tall, dark-haired man I had never seen before.

"Who is Meiser talking to?" I asked Ava. She spun around and peered out the window as well.

"Hey, I saw that guy talking to that red-headed kid earlier. He was in here," Ava said.

"Tink?"

"Huh?"

"The red-head with freckles? His name is Tink."

"His *name* is *Tink*? He must have had weird parents," commented Ava rudely.

I rolled my eyes. "It's a nickname, dum-dum." Ava and I used to be known for eating hundreds of dum-dum suckers as kids—we lovingly called each other dum-dum from time to time.

"Whatever. Anyway, yeah, they were huddled up in a corner. It all looked suspicious, if you ask me. Pria was not happy about it. She came thundering over and the guy hightailed it out of here. She can be scary."

"No doubt." I was watching as the two men seemed to get into a heated argument, and the stranger stormed into the community center and disappeared into the men's room.

"I wonder if it was..." Ava began, but I waved a hand to cut her off, and walked toward Meiser as he came back in.

"Who was that?" I asked.

"No one important." He walked past me.

Seriously?

I wondered if anyone would notice if I left and went home and climbed into bed, pulled the cover over my head, and hid until the rest of the holiday was over. We hadn't even eaten yet.

Speaking of dinner, I decided to head back to the kitchen to see if Pria had fixed the baster.

Pushing through the double doors, I didn't see anyone in the kitchen. "Pria?" I called out, looking around. I noticed someone left the fridge door open.

As I walked closer, I saw a puddle of milk seeping from under the open refrigerator door. My anger instantly flared. *Those teens! We invite them here, then they make a mess and don't clean it up. They could at least have the guts to come and tell me so I can clean it up. And who leaves a fridge door open?* I recoiled, shocked that those assumptions, accusations, and prejudices were hidden in my brain. I closed the fridge door, and my thoughts screeched to a halt.

Pria lay on the floor in a puddle of milk, her eyes wide and blank. The stainless-steel turkey baster was driven into her ear, and blood dripped down her jaw and neck, mingling with the milk on the floor.

Chapter Four

My head was throbbing to the rhythm of the sirens getting closer, to the flood of people in uniform, to the yellow tape, to the cordoning off of people into sections, to the questions—it was so familiar, like a song I heard too many times before.

Ava followed Meiser and Keith into the kitchen, her mouth hung open, and she clasped her hand over it to hold in a cry. "Pria?"

I nodded with tears overflowing.

Ava and I went to hug and leaned in the same direction and butted heads together. We both reached for our foreheads at the same time, saying "Ow," in exactly the same moment.

"Hey, you two, we are not in a three stooges' skit—could you please move off to the side," Meiser glared at us.

Ava and I stared a hole through him.

"Who are the three stooges?" I asked finally.

"What? You and I cannot be together. How old are you?" Meiser asked.

"We aren't together," I objected.

"I don't know who he's talking about," Ava said

out of the side of her mouth, "but he's the one acting like a stooge!"

I couldn't help but grin. My nerves were stretched so thin that I felt a little hysterical. I felt awful that I was about to crack up after someone had just died. I always expressed grief in an abnormal manner.

"We told you that you shouldn't invite those criminals from the city here!"

Teddy had walked back to the kitchen, removed Ava and I, went into police mode, began taping off the scene, gathered people to another room, and then began questioning people who were at the scene.

The Daltons were standing arms crossed, and Mrs. Dalton was the one who made the obnoxious comment.

"They are not criminals!" I said in an extremely immature tone.

"Well, who exactly do you think killed that poor girl? We all saw those three hooligans screaming at her," Mrs. Dalton insisted. "Then, I saw that red-headed boy leaving the kitchen right before you went back there. This is what happens when you invite criminals into the village!"

"Yo, back off! If you've forgotten already, we've had three crimes in the village in the last year alone. Walk away." Ava stood in front of me like she was my bodyguard, "NOW!"

The Daltons were not dense enough to mess with Ava when she was in protective mode.

"Thanks," I said.

"I'm sorry if I was insensitive back there. You

know I get weird when I don't know what to say," I said, hugging Ava. "I didn't mean to joke or grin, ugh."

"I know. I don't know why we're both acting like we lost a sister. We've only talked to her a few times. I know you really respected her, though," Ava said.

"She had everything and everyone working against her, and she beat the system that tries to keep the poor down. Then, she went and paid to get an education to help others get out of poverty while being able to live their truth."

"She was something else. It's really hard to believe someone wanted her dead," Ava said.

"Who will these kids have to look up to now?" I asked.

"I don't know. They look devastated." She nodded toward the corner where the teens were gathered, crying.

There was a woman with flowing, long, dark-blonde hair with purple highlights and a face of an angel sitting alone in another corner of the room. She looked completely devastated. I hadn't noticed her earlier and wondered if she worked with Pria.

"Come with me." I grabbed Ava's hand and walked toward the woman.

I bent down on my knees. "Hi, I'm Jolie Tucker, and this is my friend Ava Martinez. Are you okay?"

This seemed to tip her over the edge. "Oh!" she said, painfully, then started to weep. "I'm so sorry!" she choked out between sobs. "Hi Jolie, Pria had a lot of great things to say about you." The woman gasped and blew her nose.

"Did you work for Pria?"

"I'm Stef—Pria's partner," she reached out a shaky hand.

"The librarian who saved her?" I asked.

"She was always telling people I saved her. I thought it was the other way around. My life was so dull, very routine. Then, Pria came into my world, all full of fire and vitality. She was determined to find a way out of the streets and poverty. How can some have that grit in them, and others just stay victims?"

"I was just saying something similar to that. I've only talked to her a few times, and I can't believe how much of an impact she had on me in such a short time. She had everyone working against her, and she wouldn't give in," I said.

"That was Pria," Stef winced with a distant, dull stare into space.

"She seemed like a saint. Do you know of anyone who would want to hurt her?" I asked.

"Yeah, I don't know if you were here earlier, but three of the teens were screaming at her. She was pretty firm with them, and they didn't seem pleased," Ava said.

"That was par for the course. It wasn't a normal day unless one or more of the teens were upset with her," Stef said.

"Do you think any of them could hurt her?" Ava asked.

"It's difficult for me to believe. They always had issues, but they respected her and knew she cared for them," Stef said.

"What about the red-head they call Tink?" I asked. "Pria said he was new."

"I don't know him," Stef said.

"How is your police staff? Are they used to having to deal with this sort of thing in this village? I want the person or people responsible caught," Stef said.

"We've had several things happen over the last year, but Jolie and I were instrumental in solving the cases," Ava bragged.

"That's not necessarily true," I said, giving Ava a look.

"Will you help? I need to know that this will be solved," Stef pleaded.

I looked hard at Ava. "We'll do our best."

"Psst, Ava," I jerked my head to the side, encouraging her to follow me to the side office off the cafeteria area.

"What are we doing?"

"I want to get to a computer to start thinking about..."

Walking into the office, we saw Chief Tobias, Meiser, and Keith huddled up. They didn't know it, but they resembled a mismatched trio from an odd-couple comedy movie. Mick looked the detective role in a long trench coat with a button-up, white, crisply ironed shirt, thick locks of brown hair and a clean-cut square jaw. Keith looked like the ex-football player cop-jock who was still in great shape, but there was the chance with time, a belly may emerge. Teddy was that guy now. He was short, stocky, with a loveable belly. Although at the moment, his face was quite serious.

"Sorry, we were trying to get to a computer," Ava said.

"Why?" Meiser asked.

Ava and I glanced at each other.

"Bored," I said, shrugging my shoulders.

"Mhm," Meiser did not look convinced.

"Why are you all huddled up in here?" Ava asked.

It was weird seeing Meiser and Keith together. I'd have to get used to that. I smiled and waved to Keith.

"Happy Thanksgiving," Keith said awkwardly.

"Not really," Ava sighed.

"We're putting a call in to Tabitha to have her meet us here. I thought she was planning to come today," Teddy said, looking at me.

"How would I know?" I asked, feeling my face turn red, wondering if everyone in the village knew I was seeing her.

"Why do you need to speak to her?" Ava asked.

"You're awfully curious, aren't you?" Meiser asked.

"You shouldn't speak to me," Ava growled.

"We'll find somewhere else to go." I turned Ava around and led her away.

"Jerk," Ava barked as we left. I hoped no one heard her.

"Calm down," I said.

"What? He is a jerk! The way he treated you. You aren't forgiving him, are you?"

I really couldn't wait to get some alone time to journal about all this. I hadn't realized how much I looked forward to getting perspective on things. I needed to explore my feelings with Meiser and decide if I could get past certain things or not. Now, with this murder, I had a lot more to work through.

"Listen, since we can't get to a computer, let's go and discreetly take some pictures of people that are here that we think could have done this. We'll meet up later to make I Spy Slides and start noting some things," I said, taking out my phone.

"Oh, a reconnaissance mission!" Ava said.

We headed back out to where the crowd was and split up. I saw Tink and snapped a picture of him, then snapped several pictures of the teens, trying to be sure to get the three that were yelling at Pria earlier.

"Having trouble with your phone?" Stella had walked up behind me, startling me.

"Oh, yeah, I set it up to use my fingerprint, but I keep forgetting," I was aware as I said that it was a lame excuse.

"Depends on the phone how well the fingerprinting works," Stella said, looking away.

"How are you doing with all this?" I asked.

"Not good," she said. "I can't believe it."

"I know," I said.

"No, I mean, I really can't believe it. I know it happened, but I keep thinking I want to go talk to her about it. She's who I went to for everything." Her body started quivering. Ava subtly angled her phone toward Stella and tapped the screen. She was taking a picture! I felt a burst of anger.

I put my hand on Stella's arm. "I have no idea what all you've been through or how close you were to Pria. But I am one-hundred-percent certain that this is a situation that you could use as a reason to give up and go back to whatever your life was before. Pria would not want that for you. She would want you to keep moving forward, to find strength in yourself. Remember that rope and how you reached down inside yourself to get to the top? You have to do that now." I felt like I was channeling Pria.

"I know. I've never had to go it alone. I feel horrible because I was awful to Pria the first year we worked together. Now who will I lean on?"

"You can come to me, Stella. But I also believe you can take care of yourself. Pria was there for you, but you could have chosen a different path. You kept choosing this path."

"Thanks, I guess. I'm being a jerk thinking of myself when poor Pria is gone. And in such a violent way."

Some teens came up to her at that point and started talking.

I saw Meiser standing, looking out the window, and moved toward him.

"Penny for your thoughts?"

"I feel cursed," he said.

That was an odd statement coming from him, "Why?"

"This village was basically crime-free until I showed up last year," he said, rubbing his jaw.

"You didn't hurt anyone. Unfortunately, crime can happen anywhere."

"I know that all too well."

"You feel that way because of the job you do. I'm sure that's it," I said, trying to console him.

"Maybe."

"Not to change the subject," I began, "but I was wondering something. Obviously, Thanksgiving is canceled. There is a ton of food. Are we allowed to box some of it up and send it with the staff for the teens?"

"Let me check with Teddy, but I don't see why not. There's a ton of things sitting out in the cafeteria area. You may not be able to take what is in the kitchen, though."

"That's fine. Anything would be good," I said.

It looked to be a long night of waiting.

Chapter Five

I was out like a light when the phone jarred me out of a deep sleep. I tried to move and realized I had two cats pushed against me on one side of my body and two more cats on the other side—they had sandwiched me in. I had to wriggle my body straight out from under the covers and groggily reached for my phone.

"Hello," I whispered.

"I need you to get over here, NOW!" said a high-pitched voice that seemed familiar.

"What? Who is this?" I asked.

"What do you mean—who is it? What is wrong with you?"

"Ava?"

"Um, yeah, get over to my house, ASAP!"

Click.

I lifted my legs around my little cuddle bugs and sat at the edge of the bed, rubbing my eyes. Looking at the alarm clock, I couldn't believe it was ten a.m. Normally I was an early riser. Yesterday seemed like a dream. Well, more like a nightmare.

BZZZZZZ—a text from Ava.

Where are YOU?!!!!

On my way! Geesh!

I got up and threw some clothes on, looking at the cats still sleeping, wishing I was too. I headed next door to Ava's cottage. Walking out into the sunlight, I stretched my arms straight up toward the sky, breathing in the autumn-crisp air. My mums were still in bloom since fall in Ohio is riddled with Indian summers. I caught a whiff of the spicy fragrance that connects the mum's family ties to daisies. Despite what happened yesterday, the village was alive with families heading out to find the best sales before Christmas.

I hadn't bothered to brush my teeth or do my hair and didn't even pay attention to what clothes I threw on.

"What is so urgent I have to run over here? I was sleeping, you know?" I came to an abrupt stop. Ava's entire family was sitting casually around the kitchen with cups of piping hot coffee. Delilah and Ava were standing awkwardly. Ava looked panic-stricken, which was unusual.

"No doubt, Jolie. Seems your hair needs to be tamed, and maybe you should have put a tiny bit more thought into your outfit." Ava's mom, Sophia, grinned as she sipped her steamy brew.

"Sorry, again, I was sleeping," I said, looking down to see wrinkled tee and torn sweatpants that had black cartoon cats all over them. I didn't want to even think about what my hair looked like. I was positive it was Medusa-like.

"Hi, Jolie." Delilah smiled shyly.

Delilah was Leavensport's resident artist. She was amazingly creative and ran the Nuu Art Studio. At any given time, there were multiple craft projects going on with the kids and teens to help beautify the village—like the murals she and the teens painted on several of the shops in the village. She and Ava had been a hot item for over a year now.

"Hi," I said, still wondering why I was here.

Ava grabbed my arm and pulled me into the living room.

"Ow, stop it! What's wrong with you?" I rubbed my elbow.

"I need you to get my family out of here, like ten minutes ago," Ava said.

"What? Why?"

"Delilah stayed with me last night, and this morning at six a.m., they appeared at my doorstep. You know I sleep through everything. Delilah came down to answer the door in nothing but a T-shirt," Ava did a high-pitched whisper squeal.

"Yikes, that's uncomfortable," I said, yawning.

"You think? Delilah came barreling up the stairs, screeching at me."

"Okay, why am I here?"

"Get them out of here," she nearly yelled, breathing hard.

"I'm not going to ask your family to leave your house. Your mother already scares the bejeezus out of me," I said, walking back toward the kitchen.

"Jolie, where are you going?" Ava clipped each word.

"I'm going back to my house."

"No, you are not. You are going to help me out of this situation!"

"How do you think Delilah feels being left alone in there right now?" I asked hands on hips.

"Oh, crap!" Ava said, running to the kitchen. "Delilah, Jolie needs you and me to go over to her house for a bit."

"Why?" Thiago, Ava's dad, asked.

"Oh, uh, well, you see, what happened is," I tripped over all my words—I hadn't had caffeine yet, so my brain was struggling to come up with a good reason, "my toilet is overflowing and Ava and Delilah, well, you know—they are plumber pros." I felt the heat rise to my ears.

Ava looked completely stunned. Delilah looked like she was trying not to laugh.

"Ava, a plumber? I don't think so," her sister Lolly said. Lolly and Ava had a long sister rivalry. Ava always felt that Lolly was the perfect daughter. She fulfilled all of their parents' expectations of a wife, a perfect mother, plus she even she managed to land a job at home to bring money in while simultaneously raising her children. Lolly never passed up an opportunity to give Ava grief, either.

Lolly's husband, Theo, barked a loud laugh.

Ava, Lolly, Sophia, and I all glared at him. I'm guessing he wasn't forgiven for cheating; it was one thing for Lolly to harass her sister, but this punk better mind his manners. He promptly zipped it.

"Delilah's taught me a lot," Ava said, not looking her family in the eye.

"I'm sure she has," Ava's mom said.

"Okay, got to go, feel free to stay or leave!" Ava said, pushing both Delilah and me out the door.

"What in Hades is wrong with you? I called you over to help us, not to make us look more..." Ava started.

"More what?" Delilah stopped in my drive. "It

seems Jolie was kind enough to come to your rescue."

"I guess. Thanks." Ava wasn't often quick to thank me. I loved Delilah so much!

"Yes, thanks, Jolie. I'm going to take this opportunity to head back to my place and change then head into work. Since it's a holiday weekend, I've got some kiddos coming in for art time later, and I need to get it all set up." She kissed Ava on the cheek, then waved from behind as she walked away, her long, wavy, brown hair blowing in the breeze.

"She's the best," I said.

"Let's go in and get on your computer. I have my phone, and we can start our slides," Ava said.

"Anything to avoid your family, right?"

"You got that right!"

I talked Ava into making something in the kitchen while I showered, changed, and tamed my hair a bit.

Walking into the kitchen, I was thrilled to see scrambled eggs with cheese and some onions and peppers sizzling with some frozen hash browns in the cast iron skillet. I popped some bread in the toaster and pulled out some butter, ketchup for the eggs and potatoes, and homemade jams.

"Whoa, slicing those potatoes the other day really inspired you in the kitchen! I'm not used to you cooking," I said, setting the placemats on the island. Kitchens were my favorite place to be. I loved the comfy feel of the greens and clay-colored walls with cast-iron skillet borders at the top of the wall where it met the ceiling. Delilah helped me

create a rust-colored stucco ceiling where I hung a
pot and pan rack above the island and a bronze
mounted wall rack for more cast-iron skillets. The
additions made the space feel more rustic and
homier.

"Still don't like to cook. I need to stress-eat
though after everything that happened this
morning," Ava said, stirring her masterpiece
together.

"Remind me to stress you out more often!"

Ava turned her head and frowned.

"I loaded my pictures on your PowerPoint." She
nodded toward the table.

My jaw dropped when I saw the first picture was
of Nestle, "You saw him inside the community
center yesterday afternoon?"

"What? No, I told you I saw him outside when I
ran to get the turkey baster. I found that picture on
the web and plugged it in."

"Oh, good. I forgot about that. I'm going to add
the pictures I took of the teens and that boy Tink as
well," I said, plugging my phone into the computer.

"Why'd you take a picture of Stella?"

"Why not?"

"I really can't see her hurting Pria. She was
devastated yesterday," I said.

"Yes, but Magda told me that Stella said she
sometimes felt like Pria was pressuring her to be
trans," Ava said.

"Really? I don't see that."

"I'm just telling you what Magda told me. And
we did see Pria have a fit yesterday. No one is
completely perfect."

I ignored Ava's comment and uploaded my pictures to my laptop, then added them to some slides. I went back through who Ava had added, "Stef!?"

"Yeah," Ava grabbed a dishtowel and put it over the handle of the cast iron skillet and brought it over to scoop out breakfast for both of us.

I grabbed some teacups and the toast and brought the laptop to the island where we sat. Ava squeezed what seemed like half the bottle of ketchup onto her eggs and potatoes.

"That is so gross," I said, taking a big bite of my eggs and then slathering some butter and homemade peach jam on toast.

"Seriously, I put ketchup on my eggs, and you always have the same reaction! You've watched me eat eggs for well over two decades now and nothing changes." Ava shook her head.

"I know, but it's just gross," I said. "Your eggs are delicious, though. They don't need ketchup—that's all I'm saying!"

"Okay, why Stef?"

"The love interest is always the number one suspect. We can't rule her out," Ava said.

She had a point.

"We need to sniff out the stabby stabberton who stabbed this poor soul," Ava said with a mouthful of egg mush.

My mouth hung open.

"What's your problem?" I said, eyes bulging.

"What?" Ava scooted the stool back.

"It's not funny!" I cried.

"I know it's not funny! I wasn't making fun."

"Stabby...stabberton?" I said incredulously.

"I mean—it's gross. They stabbed her. I was making a point."

"Not funny." I clipped my words. Wiping my mouth and throwing my napkin down, I got up and began emptying the remainder of my breakfast in the garbage disposal.

"I'm sorry. You're right—I was being a jerk. She's gone—murdered violently, and she didn't deserve it," Ava grabbed my plate and took over cleaning up my mess of eggs and half-eaten toast in the sink.

"No, you are just trying to lighten the mood," I relented. "We both have our quirks—you lighten the mood at odd times, and I'm way too serious at times when there is no need to be, then I end up giggling at the most inopportune times." I now regretted the loss of my departed breakfast.

"Yeah, it'd be great if we could balance each other out. Instead, we help each other dig a bigger hole," she grinned and elbowed me in the gut playfully.

"Yep, we are the odd couple of BFF's."

"You should find a picture online of Mayor Cardinal," Ava changed the subject while shoveling her last big bite of food into her mouth.

"Close your mouth when you chew," I said, putting a hand up to block the sight.

"Why are you this way? I am so tired of you giving me crap all the time!" Ava said, finally closing her mouth. "Oh yeah, find a picture of the Daltons too! I couldn't get a picture of those two old bags."

"You really think the Daltons killed her?"

"You saw how they acted all snooty and like I'm-so-much-better-than-any-city-criminals yesterday. I wouldn't put it past them."

"Okay, I'll search for some pictures and add them. Mayor Cardinal would not get his hands dirty, though. That I'm sure of," I said, scrolling through the internet image search.

"Right, but he would hire someone—possibly Nestle. We know that to be true."

"I'll do a split pix of Nestle and Cardinal in one slide and make a note of the possibility that the mayor might hire Nestle," I said.

"I'm going to add a picture of Meiser on one slide," I said as I looked through my folder that contained pictures of him. Wow, I had so many great ones. He really is handsome.

"Okay, you have definitely lost your mind if you think your Prince Charming did this," Ava said.

"No, of course I don't think he did it. And he's not my Prince anything!" I said as an afterthought. "He was speaking to a strange man, and it looked like they were arguing. I'm going to note that. I asked him who it was, but he blew me off."

"Shocker," Ava said with a hard edge to her tone.

"Cool it," I said.

"What about Mayor Nalini?" Ava asked.

"No way!"

"I know, but Pria was lobbying against gentrification in Tri-City, and that caused some issues here in our village. I don't want to believe it either, but our good mayor has been running some backroom deals with Mayor Cardinal over the last six months," she said.

"You really are becoming like a private detective or something," I said, thinking about the way she thought through all of this and how she presented it.

"I know." Ava kept her eyes on the screen. "I'm…thinking about taking some courses in PI work."

My head swiveled around to her and my eyebrows shot up.

"What? We've been solving *real cases* this past year. Why not? It can be a little side business, and I'll even let you help. We may as well get paid for it," she said.

"You're serious?"

"Maybe. You never know what the future holds."

"There are so many suspects here," I said, scrolling through the slides.

"We should split up the list and go out and talk to each one of them," Ava said.

"Nestle?"

"Maybe not him or Mayor Cardinal. But we can do some snooping."

"I wonder if Tabitha is involved with the case," I said, referring to my therapist.

"How exactly does that work? She's a forensic therapist, right?"

"Yeah, she's spent the biggest part of her career working for the legal system in big cities," I explained. "I'm not exactly sure what happened, but she told me there was an issue with her last case that made her want to move out of the city. Teddy was looking for someone to hire that could help with the psychology of criminals since we've had an influx in crime in such a short amount of time."

"That's interesting," Ava said.

"Yeah, I think so too. Of course, we don't have the same amount of crime she's used to in big cities, so she is supplementing her income by opening a small practice to work with some clients on a personal level too. I guess Teddy can't afford to pay her a salary, so she is doing consultant work for him on an as-needed basis."

"Well, there is one place you can do some snooping," Ava said.

"I'd assume that Teddy would use her on this. I have an appointment later tonight. I'll see what I can find out."

"Yeah, I think before we start filling in notes of motives on our slides, we should go out and talk to people first, then meet back here to type it all out," Ava said.

Regretting that I'd thrown my food out earlier, I scooped the last bite of potato and egg from the skillet into my mouth and chewed, thinking. "Good idea," I said, finally. "You reminded me, I have some therapy homework to do before my session. You are going to have to go back and face your family."

"Actually, I think someone needs to go into the restaurant today," Ava said, quickly. "I know it will be slow with everything that happened yesterday, but I'll pop in and check on things and maybe do payroll."

"You know you will have to go home eventually, don't you? Plus, don't you have to go home and change clothes?"

"Nah, I'm fine in my sweat suit," she said, heading out the door and leaving the rest of the breakfast cleanup for me.

Chapter Six

Friday 11/29/19

I'm not even sure where to begin. My initial intention was to journal about how I feel about Meiser and see if I could come to any conclusions. Then there was another murder yesterday on Thanksgiving. Pria's dead. How can she be gone? I know it's strange, but I felt like she and I would have been life-long friends. I can't even believe I just wrote all of that down. How does this keep happening? I'm beginning to understand what Meiser meant when he said, "what is it that draws crime to me?" Last summer, I guess the answer was...me, sort of. I don't want to think about that whole ordeal.

I can't imagine anyone wanting to hurt Pria. She had so much going for her and had come so far. I mean, was it an accident? Was someone gunning for someone else? Oh man, was someone gunning for me? I know what Tabitha would say: "Stop making everything about you all the time."

Did Pria have hidden secrets from her time on the street? What did she say that guy's name was? Or she didn't—they called him something like Tiny—or Smalls—that's it! I wonder if her friend knows his name. I don't even know who her friend is. I need to add a slide about this guy and her friend that she moved with to the other city.

I should work through some things concerning my feelings for Mick, but it just seems so trivial now that Pria was murdered. I mean, it makes me think I shouldn't even be that upset with him. I get the feeling he isn't telling me everything. That is a big part of the problem right there. He's already broken my trust in him, and he's still holding out on me. Maybe that's my answer.

Yet, when he grabbed me, it felt like warm syrup running through my body. The feeling of warmth, safety, and love overtook me. When I was looking at my file of pictures of him, I felt like he was my guy. Like we were a couple. What sucks is I know that is also what Keith wants from me. He's been a loyal friend to me and someone I can trust, unlike Mick. Plus, Keith and I have a history together. Why can't my stupid heart just go with the right guy?

I know Tabitha keeps taking everything back to my parents—family. Isn't that what all therapists do? This is one thing I do not understand about therapy. Therapists want to drudge up all this stuff that people have already been through and survived. It seems to me that only pushes one back into that darkness. I tried to talk to Tabitha about it, but she was adamant that it wasn't true. "The reason for adult problems stems from past issues that we don't allow ourselves to face."

So, I'm supposed to write a scene that pops in my head as a little girl. I had to stop writing for a bit and close my eyes and take myself back there.

Okay, here goes. My biological father is a manipulative dirt bag. Talk about psychological manipulation. Tabitha could have a field day exploring his mind. I have no idea if he means to do it or not. I don't know him well enough to understand that.

I mean, Tabitha says a child's brain is developing until age twenty-one and sometimes beyond that. I guess everything they see and hear and experience in those younger years strongly affect how they act, react, and behave.

Whoops, not from my four-year-old self. Do-over.

Okay, here goes—why do I keep writing that? I must not want to get to the exercise of writing down a prominent scene from my past that sticks with me—so here it goes:

I'm four or five years old, and my mom and dad are recently divorced. There had been a lot of fighting when they were together, and I remember being on edge a lot. During the divorce, I spent most of my time with my grandma and grandpa, but Grandpa died when I was pretty young too.

So, back to it, I'm four or five and they're divorced. My dad get to pick me up every Sunday for me to spend the day with him. The scene that keeps running through my head is standing at the front door, looking out at the road and the driveway.

My black cat puffy coat was zipped up. I forgot I made Daddy a card with his dog, Barney, on it.

"Mommy, I have to run back to my room to grab something, can you wait by the door in case Daddy comes?"

I don't understand why Mommy always has

that look on her face when it's Daddy's day to pick me up.

I grabbed the card and put it in my Hello Kitty purse and ran back to the door.

"Got it, you can go now," I said rudely to my mom.

She put a hand on my shoulder. "He's not coming."

I jerked my shoulder away and pouted.

"Babe, he's done this the last six Sundays. You stand here, all ready to go and wait and wait. He doesn't call. It's not right. It's not fair to you. I'm sorry, he's not coming. Let's get your coat off—you've had it on close to two hours now. You have to be hot." She reached for my zipper.

"NO! Leave me alone. He's coming this time! I'm not hot. I made him a card. It's got Barney on it. He'll show up. Just go back to the kitchen or whatever," I said, tears falling down my cheeks onto one of my black kitties on the coat.

My mom was silent and walked away, turning down the hall toward the bedrooms. I heard mumbling sounds and sneaked to the end of the hall to try and hear more while making sure I could still see outside the door in case he pulled in the drive.

I heard my mom say, "She's standing at the

door waiting in her coat. She made you a card. You are three hours late. The absolute LEAST you can do is call to cancel. I'm not kidding. You need to call back and talk to your daughter NOW!"

She must have slammed down the handset because I heard a loud crash. I scooted back to the door.

I continued to stare at the road willing my father to drive into the driveway. I tried to be good when we were together and make things easy for him. He always asked me, "How's Mommy doing? Does she have any friends over during the week? Who are they?" I didn't understand why he never asked about me. It kind of hurt my feelings, but I missed him, so I let it slide.

Sometimes I tried to think about when he and Mommy were together. Was I really bad? Did it make him not want to be with me? Maybe I should say sorry?

I was starting to get sweaty, and I needed to go potty. I unzipped my coat and ran to the bathroom and closed and locked the door. I turned the water on, so it hid my crying. I splashed some water on my face and went to my playroom to play kitchen.

"I called and Ava is coming over so you two can play," Mom said, acting as if nothing had happened.

"Okay," I said, setting up my dolls and stuffed animals and getting the aprons out to put on them. Ava had drawn little cast-iron skillets on all the aprons in black marker and added a name tag for each of our workers. Ava's mama had found little cast iron key chains, and our friend Delilah took them and made them into necklaces that we'd put on when we played kitchen.

Ava came barreling in, throwing on her "#1 hostess with the mostess" apron she made. "Yay, you got our staff ready to work!"

"Yep," I said.

"Did the jerk not show up again?"

I shook my shoulders, slamming down one of our artsy menus we made together with colored-markers and grabbing the placemats we made.

"Oh well, at least we get to play kitchen all afternoon!" Ava exclaimed, picking up a Pound Puppy and saying, "Right, Ruff? Ready to work, Mr. Ruffman?"

"Rrrrruf!" She put the little white guy with black dots on him in my face.

I giggled.

Ava and I got lost in creating new recipes, ordering the dolls around, and Ava always had to fire at least three staff members every shift. A few hours had passed like nothing when the phone rang. My body stiffened.

"What time is it?" I asked Ava.

"I dunno, I don't know how to tell time," she said, brushing an old Cabbage Patch doll named Wanda's hair.

"Jolie, your dad wants to talk to you," my mom called out.

Ava and I stared at each other.

"I'll talk to him," she said, looking angry.

"Nah, I'm getting used to it," I said, dragging my feet toward the kitchen.

"Yeah," I grunted into the receiver.

"Hi baby, what are you doing?" He asked like nothing had happened.

Silence. It was a weird feeling of frustration rising through me, tears welling up in my eyes, and I felt my face turn red. I'm not sure if it was from fury or powerlessness or vulnerability or a combination?

Ugh, I came out of character. Tabitha—again, how does this help? This is so DUMB!

Back to four-year-old me:

"Nothing."

"Is something wrong?"

"Don't come for me anymore," I said, feeling a panic rise through me.

Silence on his end, then a scream came out of his mouth that sounded like someone was beating an animal to death.

I dropped the phone and began shaking all over and ran to my mom. "I made it bad," I yelled.

Ava appeared beside me. My mom ran to the phone, telling Ava to take me to the back.

Ava put an arm around me and led me back to the bedroom. I laid down crying.

"What happened?"

"I messed up again," I said.

"How did you mess up? You answered the phone," she said.

"I told him not to come get me again and he...he..." I buried my face in the pillow and started to wail.

"It's okay. You didn't do anything bad. I know you. It's his fault, not yours. Let's take a nap," Ava said, pulling the Care Bear sheets and comforter back after I got up and we climbed in bed and pulled the covers around us. Ava put her arm around me, and I dozed off to sleep.

I put my pen down and realized my face was wet. The ragged sob that was hidden in my throat erupted, and I put my head down on the desk and cried.

Why is adult Jolie crying now? I don't even care about my bio dad anymore. Great!

Oh crap, at the age of twenty-four, I could tell time. I was late for my appointment!

Chapter Seven

Tabitha's office was located in the center of the village, next to the police station, so she could easily consult as needed. Even though it was the day after Thanksgiving, it was a balmy seventy-eight degrees. One would think as it approached the winter months, and all the leaves had fallen from the trees, that the temperature would drop — typical Ohio weather. One never knew exactly what to expect from one day to the next.

Not thinking, I had put a heavy sweater on since it was chilly yesterday. I found myself sweating as I rushed into the office.

"She's running late, Jolie. Have a seat," her receptionist said with a slack-faced apologetic expression.

"It's warm in here," I said, walking over to grab a cup and fill it up with water from the water cooler.

"Yes, we've been having trouble with the heater the last couple of weeks. I've been dressing in layers."

"Have you been with Tabitha a long time? Were you with her when she worked in Tri-City or when she was with the FBI?" I asked.

"Yeah, Tabitha and I went through the training for the FBI together," Dreama, the receptionist said.

"Wait, you had to go through physical training to be a receptionist?" I asked, just as the door opened.

"It's a long story," Tabitha said, rushing into the office. "I apologize I'm running late. I was at the police department helping them with a murder case."

"Pria's case?"

Tabitha was rooting through her messages Dreama had for her and nodded her head.

"So, she *was* murdered," I said, thinking that was a dumb statement. Of course, she was murdered.

Tabitha seemed distracted and irritable. "Let's go get started with our session, Jolie."

My therapist made me a tad nervous. She had long, very tightly curled bleach-blonde hair, and her facial expressions always had a rough look to them. I had a stereotype of a therapist in my mind that they all looked apologetic in some way—like, "I'm so sorry you've had such a tough time with life" sort of look. Not Tabitha! She was muscular, sturdy, and straight-forward with every question and statement she made.

We moved into her office, which contradicted her appearance and was warm with Fall colors of rust and various shades of green everywhere. She had an oversized, rust-colored chair for clients to get comfortable, and a grass-green couch that had firm cushions for couples' therapy or hypnosis, possibly. The walls were a deep shade of terracotta. A large, thick rug of all the colors of the room on hardwood floor tied it all together. Tabitha had decorated with clay pots painted in these same colors with a southwestern pattern on them, and beautiful lush plants and flowers were all over the room, sitting on dark-wood furniture and hanging from the ceiling.

She had bookshelves filled with books that covered two entire walls. I always found myself looking over the titles. Anytime I watched TV or saw someone reading, I had the urge to try and see what it was. It was a weird quirk of mine.

Tabitha set a file down, and a few pictures fell out. The little I could see made me guess that they were pictures from yesterday, possibly including a picture of Pria after she had been murdered. I turned my attention to Tabitha, who sat in what looked to be the most uncomfortable chair in the office.

"Do you have your homework for today?" Tabitha asked.

I pulled out the brown leather journal I had bought for this purpose from my large tote I carried with me everywhere.

"Do you want to share anything from this entry, or would you like me to read it?"

"You can read the entry. Is it weird if I ask you to read it outside of the office? Or can I step out, maybe? It's weird to watch someone read what I wrote," I said, wringing my hands.

"Sure, that's why I have a little side office. I'll step in there and shut the door. There are some magazines on a rack attached to the side of my desk there. Feel free to browse through one, and I'll be right back."

I walked to the magazines, and my eyes darted over to the partial pictures that were hanging out of

Pria's file. I took a deep breath and tilted my head back to make sure Tabitha's side office door was fully closed. It was.

I grabbed a magazine and put the file in the magazine sitting in Tabitha's chair by her desk. Slowly, I opened the file to see several pictures of the man Meiser was talking to. There were also pictures of Stef and several of the teens, including Tink. There was also a picture of a man I did not see there yesterday, nor did I recognize him from the village. I ran back to my tote and fumbled through it for my phone and ran back to the desk to snap a shot of the stranger. I sorted through the pictures and pushed past Pria's post-death picture, not wanting to relive that image again. The last picture is what shocked me. It was a picture of Magda.

I heard Tabitha sneeze, and a chair scrape the floor. Hurriedly, I put the folder back on her desk, shoved my phone in my pocket, and jumped back to my chair, flipping through the magazine.

"You like horses?" Tabitha asked, walking back and handing the journal back to me.

"Never ridden before, why?" I squinted in confusion.

"You're reading *Horse and Rider*."

"Oh. I, uh, think they're beautiful creatures," I said, closing the magazine and walking it back over to the rack.

"So, what happened after your nap?"

"Huh?" I asked.

"In your journal, you stopped your scene after you and Ava took a nap. What happened after your nap?"

"Oh, right. I was running late, so I didn't finish,"

I said. "I don't remember."

"Why don't you lie on the couch, shut your eyes, and think back to that time?"

"No thanks," I said curtly.

"Why?"

"Don't want to." I felt my face turning to stone, similar to Tabitha's stare. Anger rushed from the pit of my stomach to the cheeks of my face, and I felt heat glowing off me.

"Why are you here? Why are you doing the homework, but only parts of it? You don't have to do therapy," Tabitha said.

"Honestly, I don't know. Sometimes I'm positive I shouldn't be doing this. Then other times, I know this is what I need. I've been this way my entire life. I feel so wishy-washy all the time. It's like there are two of me. I'm good at being social when I have to be, but I prefer to be alone. I don't let too many people in—not really *in*."

"Do you want to change that?"

"I feel like every time I think I want to be that person to open up, something happens to make me realize I have to protect myself."

"You may have felt differently had you not had to deal with your past experiences with your father," Tabitha said.

"Right, but that is where I get confused about therapy. All of the things that happened to me did happen. They shaped me. I don't know about everything you say about my mind developing from this age to whenever, but it makes sense. But that's just it, it all happened, and I feel the way I feel."

"So, what happened after the nap?"

"Isn't time up?"

"Sure, Jolie. Times up."

Rushing to my car, someone grabbed my arm from behind. I jerked around to find Tink.

"What are you doing here?" I stammered with a guttural sound from my throat. I'd had too many people attack me in the last year, and I didn't like how jumpy I was now.

"I was looking for you. Your friend Ava told me you'd be here."

"Why were you looking for me?"

"I have something I want to tell you," he said, breathing heavily and looking around.

"Do you know something about what happened to Pria?"

"No, I have no clue what happened to her! You don't think I had anything to do with that, do you?" Tink stepped toward me, a finger pointed right in my face. I took two steps back and put my palms up to show I meant no harm.

"I never said I thought you had anything to do with it. I *asked* you a question."

He took two deep breaths and a step back and grinned. "I'm sorry. I tend to have a chip on my shoulder. My family situation is unconventional, to say the least, and I tend to get upset too easily. Pria had been working with me on that."

"No need to explain family dysfunction to this girl," I said with my thumb pointing at my chest.

"Oh yeah, your family has issues too?" He leaned back toward me, interested.

"You wouldn't believe the crazy that is the Tucker family."

"Tell me," he said, rubbing his chin.

I felt like he should have a magnifying glass in his hand to peer into my soul. His extreme interest in my family threw me for a loop, and I shifted foot to foot, averting my eyes from him and changing the subject.

"So, you had worked with Pria the least of anyone at the community center. Is that right?"

"True, why?" He quirked an eyebrow.

"Had she shared anything with you about a guy named Smalls?"

He took a moment to think, "I would remember that name—it's like mine--different. No, but she did say that she and Stef were having some issues."

"Really? I'm surprised she would share something like that with you," I said, squinting at him. Tink bit his lower lip and looked at the sky, shifting back and forth nervously.

"Yeah, well—uh, you see, I overheard her arguing on the phone one day and asked if she was okay. That's when she told me she and Stef were fighting. Hey, I gotta go—catch you later," he said, spinning around and dashing off.

Very peculiar behavior, indeed!

Finally, pulling into my drive after what felt like the longest day ever, I dragged my heavy tote bag across the passenger seat and lugged my body out of the car. Too much emotional baggage with the journaling, the therapy session, then this episode with Tink. I was ready for bed.

"Did that kid find you?" Ava said, walking over from her front porch.

I felt my body tighten, "Yeah." I said shortly. "Um...I'm tired."

"Someone's in a mood!"

"Like I said, I'm tired."

"What's wrong?" Ava asked, following me inside.

"It's been a long two days."

"You're telling me! I ran into Betsy this afternoon at our restaurant. She brought some leftover chocolate cream pies from yesterday," Ava said.

"Ava, seriously, I'm—"

"I know, you're tired! Listen to this first. Betsy overheard the chief talking at her shop. He mentioned some guy named Smalls concerning Pria's murder."

I perked up, "Did you say Smalls?"

"Yeah, I'm assuming that's not his real name. At least I hope not."

"Pria mentioned him when we talked," I said.

"You didn't catch another name, did you?"

"I wasn't there. It was Betsy. Boy, you really do need to sleep."

"Yeah, we need to find out the real name of Smalls, though. He could be our killer!"

"Duly noted, girl. Now nigh-nigh time." She pushed me in the direction of my stairs and closed the door.

Chapter Eight

Ava and I contacted Carlos and Magda to see if they'd be up for working more hours this weekend for a little extra money. Ava had checked the books, and we typically got a spike in profits around the holidays, since people were always so frazzled, and out running around. The last thing they wanted to do is think about making food when they got home. Ava and I agreed to paying both Carlos, Magda, and Mirabelle a bit more an hour for Saturday and Sunday as holiday pay if they'd run the shop for us. Of course, they had both our cell numbers in case of questions or emergencies. Being the amazing employees they were, they all jumped at the opportunity and thanked us.

We split our "person of interest" list, each taking half. We figured the weekend was a good time to meet with people.

I had called Stef, Pria's partner, before I went to bed last night and asked her to meet me at Cast Iron Creations for breakfast. I wanted to see if Tink was telling the truth. Also, if Stef were to lie, I wanted to be face-to-face so it would be easier to tell. Plus, I'm a control-freak, it's difficult for me to leave the business knowing that either Ava or I are not there.

"Checking on us?" Magda asked.

"No, just meeting a friend for a quick breakfast," I smiled. Magda nodded her head with a sarcastic look on her face. She knew me too well.

"Magda, I know you knew Stella. Did you know Pria too?" I asked, thinking about seeing the picture in the file on Tabitha's desk.

"Knew of her, but I don't think I ever met her before. Stella talked a lot about her, though."

"Did Stella or anyone you know ever mention a guy that goes by Smalls before?" I asked.

"Smalls? No, I'd remember that." Magda shook her head, wiping down the counter and turning to get pots of coffee going.

"I'll take some chamomile tea when you get a chance," I said, walking back to the kitchen to speak to Carlos.

"Hi, Miss Jolie. Thanks again for the extra pay. This will help my family much."

"Of course! And thank you for pulling my weight today and tomorrow. You are doing okay on the Dutch baby pancakes?" I asked.

"Yes, I'm playing with the recipe, though. I've got breakfast down, but we will have so much batter left, I'm going to play with savory dishes for the afternoon rush as a special."

"That's a great idea. I would never have thought of that!" I exclaimed.

"I looked some things up on the computer last night to get inspiration. I'm also going to try a kimchi hash in the skillets for a side dish for both breakfast and lunch today."

"Wow, Carlos, you are really coming into your

own as a chef! Now, I'm worried someone will steal you away from me, then what will I do?"

"Oh, you be fine, Miss Jolie. You are an excellent cook and baker." Carlos grinned.

"Yes, but I'd never get time to breathe. It's nice having you here so we can split up the work."

"Plus, I would not leave you and Miss Ava. Too much fun here and you both take care of your employees so good," he said.

"Aww, thanks! Hey, I wanted to ask you, have you ever heard of a guy named Smalls?"

"I've never met or heard of this man," Carlos said.

"Jolie, Stef is here," Magda said through the dining-room window.

"Great, thanks. Okay, Carlos, I'm going to leave you to it, and I want to hear all about the savory dishes you come up with!"

"Of course," he said, smiling and giving me a wink.

"Hi, Stef, thanks so much for meeting me here. I was more than happy to come to you. I didn't know how you'd be."

"I had to sit down to do the planning yesterday. Pria was so young. She didn't even have a will. I decided to have a small showing at the rec center for the kids, and since that is where she spent most of her life." Stef's eyes were bloodshot. She paused to rub her face with her hands.

"I'm sure she'd appreciate that. She was always thinking about those kids—the little I knew her." I felt conflicted because I felt bad for Stef's loss, but I needed to get some answers too.

"I'm really trying to get out of the apartment.

There are too many things that remind me of her. I know I need to grieve, but Pria was so full of life, and I know she wouldn't want me to sit and wallow. Plus, I'd never tried this place. I figured it would be good for me to get out for a bit."

"Well, let me recommend a Dutch pancake that our cook Carlos has been working on perfecting. He's also doing some fabulous dish called Kimchi Hash."

"Sold," she said sipping her coffee. "Whoa, this is a delicious roast!"

"Thanks, it's Adam's special brew. He's a local in the village and makes his own coffee, beer, you name it, the kid can do anything! We buy only from him."

"Wow, must be nice!"

I wrote down our order on a pad since Magda was helping other customers and ran it back to the stainless-steel order wheel.

I pulled my blue cardigan off as I walked back toward the table, hanging it on the back of my chair. The temperature had dropped ten degrees since the day before, and the trip over had been chilly. "I have to admit I called you here to ask a few questions."

Stef took a deep breath and squared herself in her chair, facing me. "I figured that."

"Pria mentioned her past to me. She was talking about gentrification and having to move to a different city because of it. She followed a friend who hooked her up with a guy named Smalls. Does that sound familiar to you?"

"Yeah, she told me all about that," Stef shifted in her seat.

"Do you know his real name?"

"I don't," she said.

"What about the lady that Pria moved with? Do you know her name?"

"She told me, but I forget. I can go through some things when I get back home and text it to you if I find it."

"That would be great," I said.

"One last thing. Did you and Pria argue a lot?" I bit the inside of my cheek.

"Hardly ever, why would you ask me that?" Stef narrowed her eyes and looked wounded.

"The boy, Tink, said he overheard Pria arguing with someone on the phone one day, and she told him it was you." I watched her reaction carefully.

Stef didn't hesitate in her answer and looked me straight in the eye, "either Pria was lying to him, or he was lying to you."

Interesting.

Our food had arrived, and we dug into the sugary, apple-cinnamon, Dutch baby pancake Carlos had whipped up in the cast iron skillet.

I was happy I started my day with a yummy meal, and speaking to someone I liked, because I knew this next task would be unpleasant.

I drove into Tri-City, going through one of the worst parts of the city first. Even on a Sunday, I could see people huddled in corners and back alleys, making unsavory deals. Lord knows what they were selling. Men in torn, dirty clothes were walking down the sidewalk alone, yelling things out to imaginary people. One man seemed to be punching an illusory person. All of the dilapidated buildings held businesses where the owners had put steel bars onto all the windows and doors making the length of the street look like one prison after another.

I double-checked that my doors were locked as I approached a red light.

Two older women with no teeth pushed carts that carried holey blankets covered in mud stains and old mismatched shoes that looked to be heavily worn. Odds and ends of what most would put in their trash hung over the carts. One of the women looked at me with empty dark eyes. I smiled and waved. She seemed shocked that I saw her and gave me a toothless smile as she passed by me like a specter.

Ironically, I had to go through this part of the city to get to the affluent neighborhood where Mayor Cardinal lived. It was, of course, a gated community. I took a chance that he would see me, but I could imagine him turning down my visit. Mayor Cardinal was a man who made it his business to know everything about any person who got in his way. Many joked behind his back that that is how he became mayor of Tri-City.

I pulled up to the gate where a security guard stepped out of a guard shack.

"Morning ma'am, state your business," a uniformed man barked at me, his posture rigid as a board.

"Good morning, sir, I'm here for a visit with Mayor Cardinal. My name is Jolie Tucker, and I live in Leavensport Village," I said with a bit of hoarseness in my voice from nerves.

"Do you have an appointment?"

"An appointment?" I asked.

"Ma'am, is he expecting you?"

"Oh, sorry, no, he is not expecting me," I said, getting more uneasy by the minute. Why was I nervous? People visited other people without warning all the time.

"Just a moment, ma'am," the guard said, moving back into his shelter.

I saw him pick up a phone, talk for a couple of minutes, replace the receiver, and come back to my vehicle.

"Ma'am, the mayor will see you now. Do you know which house is his?"

"Yes sir," I said as the gate opened. Betsy's aunt had been friends with the mayor's wife before he was the mayor and just a city official. We had all visited one afternoon a few years back. The mayor's wife was a well-known power attorney in the city, and her family came from money.

I pulled into the drive and shook my head, remembering the street I had just gone down to get to this area. This neighborhood was only four streets over from one of the worst parts of the city. The stark difference in environments amazed me.

Stepping out of my car, I looked around at the perfectly mowed lawn, and turned my head around the neighborhood. The whole neighborhood must use the same landscaping company. Every house around his had the exact same variety of rich green grass, all cut to an identical three inches. The bushes and trees were well-manicured, and lush, full flowers of many colors and scents popped up around the entire border of the house.

The tall wooden door swung open, and Mayor Cardinal strode out in a pair of khaki Dockers, shiny wing-tips, a starched, light-blue, button-down shirt with his hair slicked back.

"What a surprise, Miss Tucker, what brings you to my neck of the woods?" He reached out a hand to shake. It was obvious this guy's whole life was shaking hands and kissing babies.

"Hello, sir, I apologize for showing up unexpectedly, and I appreciate you seeing me," I said, trying to step around him and walk into the house.

He stepped in front of me, "I'm sorry, we are getting ready to head out. What is it you needed?"

This was not going as planned. A chilly breeze made me shiver. "Oh, sure, I uh, well, I wanted to know what you know about Pria Stephens?"

"Miss Stephens, yes. Doing a little snooping, are we?" He chuckled.

"Trying to help her partner get justice for the murder of her girlfriend," I said, crossing my arms from the cold.

"Isn't that the police's job?" The mayor's upper lip twisted into a sneer.

"Of course, it is. And I am not trying to do police work. I met with her partner, Stef, this morning. Pria had mentioned someone named Smalls to me. I asked Stef about it. She's going to look into it for me, but I wondered if you'd know anything about this person?" I dodged his question about the function of the police versus a co-owner of a cast-iron skillet restaurant.

"Can't say that I've heard of a man who calls himself Smalls. I'd think I'd remember that guy," he said, rubbing his chin.

"Okay, thanks," I said, heading back to my car. I was getting sick of everyone telling me the same thing.

"That's it? You drove all the way out here just to ask me that?" He looked taken aback.

"Yep, I know you have to go. Enjoy your Sunday, Mayor," I said, hopping into my car and pulling out of the drive.

Interesting, I never said Smalls was a man.

It was late afternoon when I headed back to Leavensport. I had called Ava to see where she was, and she said she had stopped at the Nuu Art Gallery to check in with Delilah, her girlfriend. I told her I'd be there soon.

"Hey, ladies, what's up?" I said, dropping my big brown leather tote.

"Not much. I was trying to talk Delilah into taking a break for lunch with me," Ava said.

"You hungry?" I asked. This was one of the reasons Ava and I were such good friends. Neither one of us would ever turn down food, no matter how full we were. But, when we were hungry, watch out!

"Always!" Ava rubbed her stomach.

"I ate breakfast earlier, but you know me, I can always eat," I said.

"You two go. Ava, bring me something back. I have to do some things with the finances today. I've put it off too long," she said, rubbing her temples.

I knew that feeling. I was a right-brain dominant person like Delilah, while Ava was more left-brained. She enjoyed doing the books, and all the small details that go with running a business. I hated that sort of thing.

"Want to do lunch at our place?" Ava asked.

"That's where I had breakfast, but sure," I said, grinning to myself. Ava also wanted to check in on things.

"Hello, and welcome to Cast Iron Creations. I'm Mirabelle, and this is Spy. Please, have a seat anywhere," Mirabelle our hostess with the mostess gave her same spiel she said to all who entered.

"Hey Meer, hey Spy," Ava said as Mirabelle automatically lifted her hand for the high-five she and Ava always exchanged.

We sat down to talk, and Magda came bouncing up to the table. "Huh, first Jolie, now you are both here. I get the feeling you two don't think we can run this joint," Magda said.

"Nah, Jolie is a control freak. I know you all know what you are doing," Ava said, selling me out.

"Nice," I said, as Magda ran back to get us both Cokes.

"What, it's true, isn't it?"

"Like you aren't making sure things are okay, too," I said in a huff.

"Listen–" Ava started.

I put a hand up to stop her and got up, moving to the front window.

"What are you looking at?" Ava asked.

"That man over there," I pointed across the street.

"That's Nestle," Ava said, grabbing her phone.

"Oh, I didn't even see *him*. Over there." I pointed. "The man he's talking to is the strange man Meiser was with on Thanksgiving," I said.

Ava ran out of the shop.

I took a breath to yell to ask her what she was

doing but held my tongue not wanting to make a scene. She ran across the street toward the community center. The men were in the alley between the community center and Sir Scratch A Lot's veterinarian shop. I saw her peek into the community center then walk past the alley to the vet's office. She walked up the steps to the vet's, pulled on the door, which was locked, because they are closed for lunch, and came running back to our restaurant.

"What on earth?" I grabbed her arm as we went back to the table.

"I snuck a video of them," Ava said.

"Did they notice?" I asked, concerned. "I get the feeling both of those guys are trouble. You need to be careful."

"Nestle asked what I was doing. I told him to mind his own business. I'm allowed to walk where I want. One of those jerks whistled at me. They didn't know I had the phone pointed at them but held it at my leg as I walked by."

"Let's see it," I said, scooting my chair next to her.

Magda had brought our Cokes out and asked what we wanted to eat. We ordered the savory pancakes and hash. I didn't mind eating something similar twice.

"Did you get any audio?" I asked.

"How would I know? I was trying not to be noticed. I didn't stop and do a soundcheck!" Ava said pulling her headphones out and turning the video on and listening.

It was only a few seconds of tape. When she took the headphones off, I said, "well?"

"I can't make out what they are saying."

"Let me try," I said grabbing the phone and putting the headset on.

I watched it once, noticing the men seemed concerned about something but not necessarily angry.

I played it back two more times, listening closely. The third time I swear I heard one of them say, "Mick," but that might have just been in my head because I had seen him talking to Meiser on Thursday.

I squealed loudly as two hands landed on my shoulders. Pulling the earbuds out of my ears, I looked up to see Meiser looking over my shoulder.

"What are you two doing?" He asked, glaring at the phone.

"Um, I was just..." I stammered.

In a flash, Ava was on her feet, chin out, hands on hips. "Who do you think you are," she snapped, "coming into our restaurant, laying hands on Jolie, and snooping in our business?"

"I'm a customer who knows the owners and wanted to walk up to say hi before ordering. Then, I notice that you are videotaping civilians without their knowledge. So, being the detective I *also* am, I'm asking what you two are up to!"

Okay, so Meiser didn't let Ava dissuade him.

I slumped, defeated. "Okay, so we talked to Pria's partner Stef on Thursday," I began. "Pria had shared some things with me. We were looking into it. When we met up here, we saw Nestle over there. I realized that's the guy you were arguing with on Thanksgiving. Ava went to grab some video, and here we are."

Ava was gawking open-mouthed at me. Normally, she was the one to confess all. Today, we changed places.

"What?" I went on. "It's the truth! Also, I swear I heard one of them say 'Mick.' Which I believe is you! So maybe you should take an interest. Here. Listen to it," I handed the phone and earbuds to him.

"Oh, I thought they were saying 'Nicky'," Ava said.

"Probably Micky," Meiser said.

"You go by Micky?" I asked.

"No," he said, putting the earbuds in.

Ava and I stared at each other.

"Thanks," Meiser said, handing the phone to me.

"It's hers." I nodded toward Ava.

He handed her the phone and began walking toward the counter.

Ava and I looked at each other quizzically, then back at him. "Uh, excuse us, where do you think you are going?" I asked.

"To order my food."

"Wait—who is the dude calling you Micky?" I asked.

Ava nodded emphatically.

Meiser's brow furrowed. "None of your business. Drop it, Jolie."

In a split second, Ava was in Meiser's face. "You can't talk to her that way!" she growled. "What makes you think you can treat her like crap and then speak to her that way?" She shoved Meiser in his chest, causing him to stumble backward. He recovered his balance, then put both hands up.

"Whoa, Ava, I've been nothing but apologetic to her. I'm trying to protect you both right now when I tell you to drop it," he said.

"Ava, calm down," I said, grabbing her arm. She was worked up. She was breathing heavily and red in the face. She did this to my bio father several times when we were kids.

"We don't need you anyways, Mister Bigshot Detective," Ava said, gathering her things and pulling me toward the door. In an afterthought, she turned around and said, "Hey, thanks, though. I wasn't sure what my next step in the future was, but now I know."

We charged out, then I stopped outside the door.

"What?" Ava asked.

"Our food is in there. Carlos made our food. I'm going to go back and have them box it up." I reached for the door.

"Oh no, you're not." She grabbed my arm. "Let's go."

"Hey, don't pull so hard!" I broke free.

Ava was heading around to the back of the building where the alley was.

"Hey, what did you mean when you told Meiser that he helped you make a decision about the future?"

"I'm going to take those online courses to pursue being a private investigator. Also, here, I got this for you." Ava pulled a taser out her bag and shoved it at me.

"I don't want this!"

"Put it in that overnight bag you carry around everywhere. If we are going to be investigating and dealing with creeps like Nestle, then we both need to be able to protect ourselves!" She then knocked on the back door. A moment later, it sprang open, and Carlos' cheerful face poked out.

"Hey Carlos, can we get that order to go?" Ava asked sweetly. He nodded and disappeared. Two minutes later, he passed us a carryout bag and waved goodbye.

Best. Employee. Ever.

Grandma Opal was sitting in my kitchen when I got home. Unfortunately, I made the mistake of giving my mom a spare key in case I ever needed her to come and take care of my four cats. She made copies for my grandma, aunt, and uncle. Typically, they knocked, but if I wasn't home, they'd go on in and make themselves at home.

"I brought you some homemade noodles. There's a container in the fridge, and I made more and put them in freezer bags. In summary: you have four bags of noodles in your freezer." She hadn't looked up from my Vogue magazine during this entire speech.

"Thanks!"

"These girls are too skinny." She held up the magazine with a look of disgust.

"They're models. It's part of their jobs to be skinny," I said.

"It's not real. I read somewhere that they fix the pictures. Like this young lady, she can't be this skinny and have boobs that big," Grandma said.

"I mean, yeah, she can," I said, not feeling comfortable with this conversation.

"How?" Grandma's lower lip stuck out.

"I mean, she could have had, you know, work

done," I said, nodding toward the girl's breast.

"You mean a boob job? You'd think that wouldn't be fair play to hire models who are having work done on themselves. Why not use real women in these magazines? That's the people who give them money. Real women who work day in and day out to earn that money," she said, slapping the magazine closed.

"That's a good point," I conceded. "Did you need something?"

"Oh yeah–Keith was looking for you," she said, taking a sip of tea she made herself.

"And he called *you*?"

"No, he called your home number and I answered. He said he tried your cell, but you didn't pick up," she said.

Ava gave me crap all the time about keeping my landline. She swore I was the only twenty-something in the world who still had a landline. She's so dramatic.

"He wanted you to call him as soon as possible," Grandma got up and grabbed her stylish Coach purse. She met me halfway as I bent down and she reached up to give me a kiss. "I'm off to my Pilates class."

"You don't look dressed for Pilates," I said.

"Got my yoga pants and tank top in my bag in the car," she said.

Now my grandma was a short lady at four foot ten, but she was Well-endowed in the bosom area. It was probably the reason why she took offense to a model getting a "boob job." I shook my head at her antics, and she closed the door. Then I picked up the phone.

Keith answered on the first ring. "What's up?"

"Jolie, I figured you'd want to know. They arrested someone for Pria's murder."

I was stunned. "Who?" I asked.

"A man named Steve."

Chapter Nine

I'm happy to get to choose what to write about for this homework session.

After spending time exploring why I'm the way I am in therapy, I realized that my relationships have been doomed from the beginning. Keith and I had flirted for as long as I can remember. We "played" boyfriend and girlfriend when we were in kindergarten and first grade. I remember telling him he was my husband.

We dated in high school for close to three years, but then my stepdad, Mike (who I call my real dad) got prostate cancer, and over the course of a year, he slowly died. (BTW: Tabitha—when you hear me refer to 'dad' or 'real dad' that is Mike my stepdad; whenever you hear me say my bio dad or biological father—that is, well—my biological father). Anyway, when my dad died, I was broken inside. He and I just understood each other.

He always said I was an anomaly because I was planning my future at such a young age. Plus, he knew my entire family and that they are all a bunch of nutjobs—lots of drama and dysfunction, but I've always been a straight shooter.

I remember the night he died. He had most of his family and friends around his hospital bed. He was saying something special to everyone. His sister said, "Mike, Jolie is here. You haven't said anything to her yet." He shook his head, looked down at his comforter, and grabbed my hand and said, "Jolie and I don't have to say things to each other. We just know." And he was right. I had gotten so used to not trusting most people, but especially men—then Dad came into my life and changed all that. And then, he died.

I couldn't be with Keith. We were suddenly from different worlds. He was into prom, football, and all that high school stuff. All things I no longer cared about. So, I ended it and spent most of my time in class or my room the rest of high school. I didn't really come back to life until Ava and I began really planning for our restaurant and working on getting it up and running.

When Mick Meiser came into my life, I was skeptical and tried to keep a distance. I could tell he was interested in me, and I can't help saying I was definitely interested in him. I know you'll ask me my first negative thought about him. I remember. It was that 'this guy is ten years older than me; he just wants me for my age.' You know, you always hear about older men wanting younger women. That's what I thought. With time, I realized he and I have a lot in common. Also, even though I'm younger, I've had an older spirit. I was an only child after all and grew up more around adults than kids.

Well, I've shared with you the lies Meiser told. Again, it comes down to trust. I have to say, I feel like you are pushing me to trust people in spite of *how many times people give me reason not to trust them. I could be wrong, but that's how I feel. I'm not sure I'll ever be an extrovert or that I really want to be. I enjoy being alone, reading, watching T.V., hanging with my cats. I'm close to my family and Ava and the people I work with. I know everyone in the village. No, I'm not out all the time or texting, calling, and scheduling outings. But that's because I'm most comfortable being alone.*

Anyway, that's where I am right now. Like I said to you before, Keith is the one who was honest with me about Meiser. I can't help but be a little angry with him even though logically, I know it's not his fault. I don't have the same feelings for Keith that I do for Meiser. But I wish I did. I feel like he's safer. I feel like that's who I should be with. But, my heart...

I was on my way to meet with Keith at Chocolate Capers for something sugary.

"Hey Betsy," I said, walking in and looking at her display case full of chocolate brownies, mini cakes, cupcakes, full-sized cakes, cookies, and candies. The smell was divine.

"Hello, beautiful," Betsy said in her cheerful way. Betsy was one of those women who possessed natural beauty. She had long flowing, wavy red hair, hazel eyes, and I never saw her work out, but she always looked to be the picture of health. I have witnessed her eat a ton of chocolate, though! Truthfully, I wanted to hate her, but she was so kind and giving that I treasured her—not to mention she was so laid back about most everything.

"You always know how to cheer a gal up," I said,

reaching for a sample. Betsy always had samples sitting on the counter. This one looked to be a chocolate bar, dense with coconut, nuts, something else that was white, and I tasted a hint of cayenne. "Wow, this is delicious."

"Double-chocolate sizzling crunch is what I'm thinking of naming it. I'm playing with names still. I'm trying to see what people think of it first. Feel free to name it and put your choice here in the basket. If I choose your name, then you will get a dozen for free."

"Heck yeah!" I reached for a pen and wrote my thoughts down.

"Want a cup of tea?" Betsy asked, reaching for my pumpkin blend.

"Yeah, do you still have your pumpkin blend?" I asked before I saw what she was doing.

"Sure do, want a cup or little teapot full?"

I loved that Betsy gave the option of cups or teapots. She had the cutest little china teapots she served the tea in. I had thought about doing that, but we never had enough people order hot tea to make it worthwhile.

"I think Keith likes that blend too. Let's get a teapot to share," I said.

"Are you two back together? I see you with him a lot more lately."

"We're just friends. Although you're right, I have been spending more time with him the last several months."

"With who?" Keith said, walking up, bending over, and kissing me on the cheek.

He looked handsome in his uniform, but the kiss made me uncomfortable, and I squirmed away from him.

"Nothing! Betsy has her pumpkin blended tea," I said.

"Let's share a teapot," he said, finishing my thought.

I grinned and nodded at Betsy.

"Want a sweet treat too?" he asked. "It's on me."

"You don't have to do that," I said.

"I want to do it. What are friends for?" He reached across the table for my hand.

I let him hold my hand for a few moments before pulling it away. "Thanks, Keith."

"Betsy, can we get two brownies too?" he yelled over the counter.

"Coming right up," she said.

"How'd you know I'd want a brownie?"

"I know you better than you think I do," he said, waggling his eyebrows at me.

It made me laugh.

"Thanks for letting me know about that guy Steve. Do you know if he went by the nickname Smalls, by chance?" I asked.

"His last name is Smalls," Keith said with one eyebrow raised.

"Okay, that makes sense. It seems like all these kids that come from the streets have nicknames, so I just assumed Smalls was a nickname," I said.

"How do you know him?" Keith asked as Betsy brought out our pumpkin tea and chocolate brownies.

"You two enjoy," she said.

Keith took the teapot and poured me a cup first, then him. He added a dab of cream to my cup and handed me two sweet-n-lows. What was wrong with me? Things seemed so easy and natural with Keith. Plus, he never held back. Meiser would not even be talking to me about this.

I proceeded to summarize my conversation with Pria the day we met about gathering for the holiday.

"So, this Smalls guy had a reason to want her dead," he said, taking a huge bite of his brownie. He had a clump of chocolate on his chin.

"You've got—" I reached across the table, and he grinned, making some of it fall to the floor. "Wait, no, now it's," I said, and we awkwardly reached for the crumbs on the floor at the same time and almost smacked heads together.

We exploded into laughter just as Mick walked in and up to our table.

"What's so funny?" He did not look the least bit amused.

"Nothing, it's dumb. I had chocolate on my face and—oh never mind, man. She and I—she just... has always made me laugh." Keith wiped his face and stared up at Meiser.

The lighthearted atmosphere was instantly replaced by thick tension.

"Sharing a pot of tea, huh? Are you two on a date?" Meiser asked.

This angered me. "We're having a snack and chatting." I crossed my arms and glared at him.

"So, a date," he said walking out the door.

I couldn't stop myself from running after him. He was much taller than me, so his long strides got him further down the block faster than mine. Finally, I caught up to him in front of his restaurant, M&M's, and grabbed him by the forearm. He whirled around and glared down at me.

"Hey, who do you think you are?" I demanded. "You don't own me. You don't control me. You don't get to decide when or if I forgive you. You are the one who screwed up, not me! So, stop walking around the village where I grew up, acting as if you control me."

I saw his lips thin out and twitch as he stared me straight in the eye. He didn't look happy. I waited what seemed an eternity for his comeback. Nothing. He...just...stared.

"Well?" I yelled. Then I was done, abruptly turning to head back to Chocolate Capers.

Meiser grabbed my arm and spun me around and pulled me into his chest. He raised my chin and planted a kiss on me. I felt my weight lean into him, and my body let go of the tension that was just there. One of my hands made its way into his thick head of hair, and I willed my other hand not to slide down on his backside.

He pulled back and gazed at me again. This time he had a longing look.

I jerked away and ran down the sidewalk and escaped back into the shop, face blazing.

It was Monday morning, and I was prepping for the day in the kitchen of Cast Iron Creations. I felt horrible. Not only had I run out on Keith, then kissed Meiser, but then I went and told Keith I had to go. He was not a happy camper.

"I thought you were headed to Tri-City today to look into some paperwork on the gentrification issue before we meet up later about the case," Ava said.

"No need," I said, chopping parsley for the soup I was preparing for dinner service. "Keith told me they arrested a man named Steve for Pria's murder."

Ava whirled around and gave me an incredulous look. "Uh, yeah, exactly. You need to keep up with the news. Steve Smalls was killed in his cell last night."

Chapter Ten

Later that morning, we reconvened at my cottage. We had some of the Tucker family and the Martinez family come in and take over the restaurant since Magda had classes, and Carlos had had to cover way too much for me. I was still reeling from what Ava told me about Steve Smalls.

"Well, I still think Nestle has something to do with it. He's just hinky," Ava said, squinting her eyes and lips into a funny expression that contradicted her biting tone.

"Agreed. I wish Meiser would tell me who that strange guy is," I said, thinking about that kiss again and feeling my face turn hot.

"Thinking about your make-out sesh in the middle of the street?"

My face caught fire and my mouth opened and closed like a fish, but no words came out.

"That's right, I know," Ava said smugly. "I'm sure most of the village knows by now. Your Aunt Fern saw you two. She was across the street at Buzz Cuts Barber Shop," Ava said.

"What on earth was she doing at a barbershop? She goes to Nelly to get her hair done."

"Flirting with Buzz is my guess," Ava said, elbowing me in the side.

"Great!"

"Stop being a slut bag and people won't see it," Ava said simply.

"I'm no slut bag!"

"If the bag fits," Ava laughed. "Would you calm yourself down? You are way too easy to get worked up. I'm messing with you. You're a woman who had a hot, hunk of man pushing himself on you. You had a moment of weakness, that's all."

"Right? It's true. But I want to call Keith and have him come over so we can finish our talk about Steve Smalls. Plus, I need to apologize for my behavior last night," I said.

"Why? You two aren't dating. It's just like when Bradley was all up in my business because he was into me, but I wasn't into him. It's his problem, not yours. Guys say dumb stuff like 'Oh, she's leading me on.' What, I'm breathing therefore I'm leading you on? They don't know how to take a 'no,' yet that's somehow a woman's fault?" Ava was ranting.

"I'm calling Keith to have him come over. You're staying," I said, punching his name in my phone to call.

"Hey Keith, sorry about last night. Ava's here. Can you pop over really quick? We have a theory."

I put my phone in my pocket. "He's on his way."

A few minutes later, Ava opened the door for Keith. "Hey, man."

"Hey, Ava, how are you?" He grabbed her and gave her a big bear hug.

"Good, we haven't hung out in quite a while," she

said. Growing up, those two used to play flag football all the time. Once I broke up with Keith in high school, Ava hung more with me than him. I've always felt like a jerk for that.

"We can go play some flag football right now, Tex. I'll still beat the crap out of you," he bellowed.

"Huh-uh Pack, you wish you could beat me!"

That was some inside joke about Dallas Cowboys and the Green Bay Packers. I've never been a sporty lady—so I didn't completely get it.

"How about both of you Tex Packs come in here so we can talk," I said.

They gave each other a grin and rolled their eyes.

I hugged Keith when he came in and whispered sorry in his ear.

"No apologies necessary. We should talk sometime, though. Just you and me," he said.

I nodded in agreement. "So, Ava and I think Nestle is involved in all this."

"Okay," Keith said skeptically.

"If this guy Steve Smalls killed Pria, then ended up dead—someone with a lot of power arranged that," Ava said.

"And you both think that is Nestle?"

"I mean, think about all the underhanded things he did last summer. Nothing stuck. He got a slap on the wrist. That seems like a lot of power to me," I said.

"I don't know," Keith said.

"Well, I have an idea," I began.

Ava's phone buzzed. "Oh, crap!"

"What's wrong?" Keith asked.

"More family drama. My idiot brother-in-law—

which I wish was soon to be my ex-brother-in-law," Ava said, grabbing her purse. "I'm sorry, guys. I have to go put a family fire out." She came over and hugged me, then Keith, and took off.

"What's that all about?" Keith asked.

"Supposedly, Theo cheated on Lolly. They've been separated for a bit is what I understand. They came here for the holidays with the kids and the parents to try and work it out. Doesn't seem like it's working out," I shrugged my shoulders.

"*He* cheated on *her*?" Keith wondered.

"Right? That's what I said. What has the world come to?"

"So, what's your plan?"

"Right, so I'm thinking about a way to confront Nestle today—he's pretty easy to get hot under the collar. He can't seem to stand me," I started.

"I already hate it. You said it yourself. He's not safe."

"You didn't let me finish. You follow me. You call me, and I'll ad-lib something so it sounds like I'm talking to someone. I'll head to the community center and you follow Nestle. If I'm right, he'll follow me there and have an agenda," I said.

"Still hate it."

"I know, but there's more to this. Someone had Smalls killed. How on earth could that happen to someone recently put in jail while they're still under watch until trial?"

"That's what we are all trying to figure out."

"Then let me help you," I said.

"And after all this is over, you and I sit down alone and talk?" he asked.

"Yes, I promise."

I had done a bit of investigating to figure out where Nestle would be. I had to get a bit creative, but I called Mayor Cardinal's secretary and pretended to be an associate for Mayor Nalini saying he needed to speak with Nestle immediately. I hoped it worked. She seemed to believe me and told me she'd get the message to him.

I sat in my car, texting Keith while waiting. He was close by at the station doing some paperwork and I was sitting outside the credit union. I started reading my new Heather Blake mystery on my phone while continuing to watch for Nestle. Three chapters in, and I saw him get out of a car with expensive-looking shades and one of those flat caps on his head.

I grabbed my tote and quickly texted the thumbs-up emoji to Keith to let him know I saw Nestle. This should cue him to get in a position to spy on Nestle and me. I headed toward Nestle while putting my head in my tote, pretending to look for something and smacked hard into his side.

"Geesh, I'm so sorry," I said, looking up as if I had no clue who I had run into.

"Of course, it's you," Nestle said in a flat, hateful voice.

"Oh, sorry, what are you doing back in our village? I thought you despised all of us," I crossed my arms.

"It's a free country. I can go wherever I want. And, it's none of your business, blondie," he said, pushing past me.

Why wasn't Keith calling me? I grabbed my phone and texted again.

"OW!" I yelled, falling over and purposely emptying most of the contents of my tote.

"You really are a klutz, aren't you?" Nestle said, continuing to walk away. What a complete jerk. He wasn't going to help me. Luckily my phone rang, and it was right by his foot.

"Ugh, my ankle. You're the last person I'd want to ask for help, but can you please help me? Hand me my phone and help me to that bench and I'll let you be," I pleaded.

He looked like I asked him to do the worst thing on earth, but he grabbed the phone, practically threw it at me while I was on the ground, and bent down, hastily throwing things in my tote.

"Hello, what?" I said into the phone. Keith waited silently on the other end for me to complete my performance.

"Slow down!" I continued.

"What do you mean you found it at the community center? That can't be. That guy Smalls was the killer," I could feel Nestle's eyes burning a hole through me.

"Well, it's still a crime scene. I still have a key, so I'll head over there tonight around midnight when no one will see me to grab it, then I can give it to Detective Meiser tomorrow. Okay, thanks, bye." I said all this while tilting my head away from Nestle and pretending to whisper, while wanting him to hear. I felt I deserved an Oscar for best actress.

Nestle had everything thrown in my purse and was purposely waiting to hear my phone call. We had him. Of course, he pretended to be waiting to help me to the bench. Yeah, right. Like he cared about my fake ankle injury.

"Everything okay?" he asked, helping me to my

feet as I pretended to limp to the bench.

"Yeah, just some unfinished business, but I'll take care of it." I sat down gingerly. "You can go now. I'll call someone to come get me."

It worked, I texted Keith. Now, poor Keith had to tail him through the next few hours until he preyed on me at the community center.

I went home and took a long nap since I would be out late tonight. I set my alarm and got up and dressed head to toe in black. I think Ava wanting to become a PI was rubbing off on me. I took a deep breath, petting the kitties and telling them I loved them. "Wish Mama luck," I said as I headed out the door. They yawned lazily and went to sleep. So happy they worried about my well-being.

When I arrived at the community center, I instinctively looked around, trying to assess the situation. This was a really stupid idea. Too late now. I went through my tote and got the key ready to use. Ava had given me a taser to take with me.

Heading into the community center, I felt the small hairs on my neck stand up. The village was quiet, as though a dark blanket lay over it as the villagers slept. I hadn't given much thought to the fact that the last time I was here, a woman I admired and respected had been violently murdered. Actually, I hadn't allowed myself time to grieve for Pria. I just jumped right into work and investigating. I always did this.

I realized I was standing outside the door too long and used the key to go in. I ducked under the police tape and moved from the cafeteria into the kitchen using the flashlight on my phone.

I stopped before walking into the kitchen. I did

not want to go in there.

I heard a wheezing sound on the other side of the swaying kitchen door and turned to leave when the door smacked into me. I stumbled back, falling into a cafeteria table. My phone and the taser flew out of my hands. I moved my head around; the flashlight of the phone was still on and shining past me. I leaned to get up when the intruder jumped on me. He had a ski mask on, and I heard that wheezing sound again.

"Get...off...me!" I screamed as Nestle lifted something sharp and shiny into the air and drove it downward, toward my head. I jerked my body and kneed him hard and twisted just in time to avoid the blade slicing toward my face.

I must have got him good because he rolled to his side as I did the same. I began breathing hard and panicking, wondering if anything was broken. I felt him moving toward me, and I got to my knees, crawling on the table toward the taser or the door— whichever came first.

Nestle grabbed my foot and pulled me back to him. "Where do you think you're going?"

"NOOOO!" I screamed bloody murder. I saw the glint of the weapon rise above his head again. I knew I wouldn't be lucky enough to get away twice. The faces of my cats, Ava, my family, and Mick all flashed before my eyes as the knife whistled down. I squeezed my eyes shut and felt a heavy jerk but no pain. Had I been stabbed? Would the pain come later? When I opened my eyes, the lights were back on and Keith was partway across the room in pursuit of Nestle.

Seconds later, Keith came back. "He got away. I think he knew I wouldn't leave you here to chase him. Hey, can you sit up? I'm calling an ambulance."

"No! Go after him! Don't let Nestle get away," I yelled.

"That's not Nestle," he said.

Chapter Eleven

It was Tuesday morning, and I was home in bed sleeping in. I awoke to my landline ringing, and I assumed Ava or Keith or possibly my entire extended family were downstairs because the phone was answered before the first ring finished.

I sat up, reliving the events of the last five days. I still couldn't believe that my attacker wasn't Nestle. After Keith had literally saved my life, he wanted to call an ambulance, but I talked him into helping me up so I could see if anything was broken. I was stove-up and bruised but otherwise fine.

I finally talked Keith into explaining what he meant by "that wasn't Nestle." He told me he followed Nestle, and he was positive he was heading toward the community center, but then he went right past it and met someone in front of the hospital. He finally revealed that Nestle met Tink in front of the hospital. He was so caught up in watching Nestle, he forgot to check on me. Thank goodness he remembered.

But the question was how did the intruder know I was there? I was still sure Nestle was somehow tied into all this.

I pulled myself out of bed, checked the clock, took a shower, and got dressed.

As I got closer to the kitchen, I smelled grease, coffee, and toast. I was right in that most of my family and Ava were all in the kitchen. My cats had abandoned me for the family, or more likely, for the bacon.

"Hey, Sunshine," my mom said. She used to say that to me as a kid, but every time she was worried, she'd say it again.

"Tabitha called earlier. She heard about what happened to you last night and wanted to check in. She said if you need her to call her," Grandma Opal said.

"Thanks," I said, grabbing a cup of tea and scooping bacon, eggs, hash browns, and toast onto a plate.

"Someone's feeling better," Aunt Fern said.

I glanced at Ava. "Hey, you're quiet this morning." I devoured a piece of bacon in one bite.

"I'm glad you're okay. Keith told me about what he witnessed," Ava said.

I wasn't used to seeing her so shaken.

"What exactly did happen?" Grandma Opal asked.

I shook my head, looking at Ava.

"Nothing much, Mawmaw. Just Jolie snooping and getting into more trouble," Ava said.

She had always called my grandma Mawmaw, ever since we were kids.

"Come on now, give us the deets," Aunt Fern said with a fanatic-like shine in her eyes. I'm sure she was concerned about me in her own way, but getting the inside scoop to gossip about with the ladies in her card club later was at the forefront of her mind. I wasn't planning on sharing the events with all them. It would turn into completely having to relive that scene—which I was not up for.

My mom, Patty, swatted her. "Leave her be."

"I'm going to take this upstairs and finish eating. I think I will call Tabitha and see if she can fit me in today," I said, heading up to my room for some quietude and privacy before calling.

"How are you doing, Jolie?" Tabitha asked at our appointment a few hours later.

"I'm okay, I appreciate you calling to check on me and offering to get me in today," I said.

"Of course, what you went through was traumatic. It sounds like you've had other encounters like this in the last year," she said, getting ready to take note of my many flaws.

"Yeah, I can't quite recall when my boring existence turned into this dangerous lifestyle," I said grinning.

"There's nothing funny about almost dying. And not just once, but several times within a brief span of time. Do you think you have a death wish?"

I laughed out loud. Maybe I was beginning to lose it. "I don't want to die. I mean, I know I will someday, but I'm surely not trying to die, Tabitha."

"Then why do you keep inserting yourself into these types of situations? I mean, that's what the police are for," she said, writing down some notes. "You just said it yourself—a dangerous lifestyle. Adults choose their lifestyles."

"I mean with Ellie, it was my grandma who was a suspect. I couldn't count on the people who wanted to put her away to take care of it. I didn't have a choice," I said.

"You always have choices," she said.

"I never seem to have that luxury." I crossed my arms.

"Not a luxury, just the truth—about all people."

"Right, and I don't help my grandma, and she's still in jail today unless it killed her to be in there. Meanwhile, the real killer runs free." I rolled my eyes. "That doesn't sound like a choice to me."

"How do you know that is what would happen? You are not omniscient. You always wait and expect the worst. You 'what if?' everything. It's okay not to take on everything. You can step back and let others take care of themselves."

"Do you know if Nestle is involved with Pria's murder or with Smalls being killed in jail?" I asked her directly.

She seemed taken aback and caught off-guard, "I-I don't know for sure. The police are looking into it."

"So, you know who Nestle is, then. He is a suspect," I said.

"I never said that," she said, "now let's get back to you."

I rubbed both hands up and down on my face. I was depleted physically, mentally, and emotionally.

"What? Use your words, Jolie."

I laughed again and saw the frustrated expression on her face, "I'm sorry. I'm not laughing at you. My teachers used to say the same thing to me. What do you want me to say? What will make you happy?" I pleaded.

"I'm not looking for you to do or say the right

thing or the wrong thing. Just say what you are thinking and stop trying to please me," she raised her voice.

"I feel like you are treating me like I'm some sort of puzzle to be solved. It's not that easy. I love my family so much. I'd do anything for them, but I'm not like them. I'm like the black sheep of the family. They love me, but I can't relate to them, and they can't relate to me."

"Good, keep going," Tabitha said.

"My bio father messed me up. Maybe it's what you said—I was still developing, and it caused me to act and react a certain way. But that's who I am now. I can't change any of that. I feel like you want me to change it. I don't know how." I slouched on the chair, feeling defeated.

"No one can change what's been done, Jolie. It's when we face it head-on and make decisions about how to move forward that we get our life back. And those decisions are yours alone to make. You can choose to close yourself off and to never be in a relationship again. I'm not saying there is anything wrong with that choice. I think you can be an introvert, private, and enjoy time alone and that it's not an unhealthy thing. If you are closing yourself off from something you want to try because of things that happened in the past, then that is what is unhealthy," Tabitha said, leaning her elbows on her knees.

"And that's what you think I'm doing," I said.

"I don't know. That's not for me to decide. I'm just trying to get you to face some things head-on and deal with them so you can make better-informed decisions. I feel like you think I'm your enemy sometimes. I feel like you get defensive against me."

"I'm sorry. I don't mean to be difficult."

"You don't have to apologize. It's therapy. It's not meant to be easy," Tabitha said. "I think we should keep our next appointment too and discuss what you wrote in your homework journal then."

"Sure thing," I said, heading out the door.

I was getting ready to head to Chocolate Capers for a chocolate treat when Tabitha came running out.

"Jolie, you left your scarf," she said, running it to me.

"Oh, thanks," I said, wrapping it around my neck since the temps were now in the low thirties.

"Also, um, do you know Teddy well?" she asked casually.

"Sure, we've been friends since we were kids," I said.

"Do you know if he's dating anyone?"

"I'm not completely sure. Sorry," I said, turning to head to my car.

"You can't get enough of me," Betsy bellowed when I walked into Chocolate Capers.

"Mmm, more like the chocolate," I giggled.

"Okay, I'll take it," she said, handing me her plate of samples for the day.

"I didn't get to finish my brownie the other day," I said, pouting.

"I noticed: you are the *taste* of the town yourself," she wiggled her eyebrows at me.

"Gross! Does everyone know?"

"Your Aunt Fern saw," she said, cocking her

head sideways in a what-do-you-think look. "Here, take a brownie on me."

"No way," I said, reaching in my tote, searching for my wallet.

"Seriously, you need some free chocolate after all you've been through lately."

"You're the best. Don't tell Ava—you know she gets jealous," I grinned, and Betsy cracked up.

"Now, you know I'll tell her!" She got an odd sparkle in her eye, looking over my shoulder.

I turned and smacked my brownie right into Meiser's white button-down shirt. He jumped back and attempted to brush brown crumbs off his shirt. I grabbed a napkin and began wiping the thick frosting into his top.

"What are you doing?" He asked incredulously.

"Trying to help," I said.

"Here, you two—two brownies on the house. Cup of tea and coffee coming up—I've got something in the back that will help with the stain," Betsy said, grabbing two more brownies and handing them out to us, then grabbing coffee and hot water with a tea bag.

"No way, this is not all free," I said, reaching for my wallet.

Meiser handed her a $20 over my head, "keep the change."

"Whoa, thanks!" Betsy ran to the back.

"You didn't have to do that. I'm the one who ruined your shirt," I said flushed-faced.

"I never said I wouldn't have you reimburse me for the shirt." He smiled.

Aye yai yai! Why does he have to be so

handsome and charming? Working to seem professional, unlike what my heart and hoo-hah felt, I opened my wallet. "How much?"

"Fifteen hundred dollars," he said, holding out his hand.

My jaw dropped.

"What can I say? With a name like Milano, I only buy handmade Italian clothes." His hand was still waiting for reimbursement.

"Take it off," I said.

"Here?" He asked, playing along.

"Yes, I'm sure between my mom, Grandma Opal, and my Aunt Fern, they can find a way to get the stain out. So, hand it over," I said holding my hand out.

He threw his head back, laughing out loud and slapped his knee.

"Yeah, what you just did would be nothing compared to what it would look like when those three got their hands on it!" He had tears welling up from laughing so hard.

I wasn't sure whether to be offended and defend the women of my family or laugh with him. I paused.

"You're right! It would be tie-dyed or something more tragic," I laughed.

"Or there would be holes throughout the shirt from chemicals they would try," he said.

"It could be entertaining?"

"This is true. It is more than likely ruined. I have a gym tee in my car. Let me run out and change it, and you and your clan can do your worst," he said, heading to his car, which was parked directly in front of the shop.

I watched as he unbuttoned his shirt, fantasizing that we were alone, and I was doing the unbuttoning. For a guy that's been struggling with MS lately, he was in great shape. I was happy to know he was still going to the gym and taking care of himself. He pulled a tight tee over his head, which made his dark brown locks all messy. I inhaled deeply and let out a breath of satisfaction.

"Enjoying the show?" Betsy asked.

"Er–I'm––uh,"

"I'll head to the back again—forget I'm here—unless a customer comes in," she said, squeezing my shoulders and heading to the back.

Great, now I forced my friend into hiding.

"So, that was sarcasm, right?" I asked.

"What?" Meiser asked, sitting and taking a gulp of his coffee, then a bite of his brownie.

"The shirt doesn't cost that much, does it?"

He stared stony-faced at me for a moment, "Nah, I got it at a thrift store for something like four bucks."

"Funny," I said in a not-at-all-funny-tone.

"So, are you with Keith?" he blatantly asked.

"What?"

"You heard me," he said.

"I know. We're friends."

"How close of friends?"

"Close," I said.

"But *how* close?"

"What do you mean? I said we are close friends, that's it," I said in a clipped tone.

"Are you dating? Because the other night sure looked like a date."

"We're not dating."

"That's good to know. Also, you may be upset to learn that I let him have a piece of my mind after hearing about you getting hurt the other night. You are still banged up," he said, reaching toward my bruised arm, and the reddish swollen mark on my cheek from the jerk who threw a punch at me.

"Don't confront Keith, Mick," I said.

"I don't want you hurt."

"Listen, I know we kissed the other night. You kissed me," I started.

"You didn't seem to mind, and you didn't push me away," he said, reaching for my hand.

I pulled my hand back, "No, I'll admit that I'm struggling. But I keep telling you I'm not ready to try again. If you are serious about there being a possibility for us, then you have to give me the time I need to sort through things."

"I understand," he began.

His look said otherwise. I glared at him in a way that let him know I knew he didn't get it.

"No, I get it, I promise I do. I'm not trying to make things difficult for you," he took a breath and blew it out. "How do I explain this? Listen, I'm ten years older than you. I'm not old by any means, but I've got MS. I'm dealing with it. I'm ready to be with you. I don't want anyone else. I'm trying to respect what you're telling me, but you are always around."

"Sorry, I'm always around the village where I grew up and where I co-own a restaurant," I said, rolling my eyes and clenching my jaw.

"See that? And you're cute, and stubborn, and hilarious, and smart, and a klutz. You're just...YOU. I don't know why I feel the way I do for you, but I've never felt this way about anyone before. And I've been in serious relationships. I feel a connection to you. I don't want to wait. What can I say?"

"Well, that's too bad. It's a two-way street. I'm not asking you to wait for me, either. You have to live your life. I need time. I'm just beginning to figure some things out."

"Why do you get to do it with Keith and not me?"

"Because I have history with Keith. And, no, I'm not just talking about dating him. We've been friends since we were toddlers. We grew up together. Our crew was there when he broke his arm. He was there for me when my dad died. He's the one who tells me the truth whether I want to hear it or not," I said.

"You mean about me."

"That's one example."

"I'm sorry," he said again.

"I don't expect you to tell me you're sorry anymore. If you want this to work, then you have to be honest with me. I don't trust people easily. You put a barrier between us with that lie," I said.

"But it wasn't a complete lie. I did change my name from Milano to Meiser. I had a reason to do it."

"Why can't you tell me what the reason is? Also, who was the man you were arguing with? How does he know Nestle? How do you know Nestle? You say you want us to be together. So, give me a reason to trust you again by telling me what's going on."

"I will, someday, I promise," he said, shaking his head.

I felt like we were on a merry-go-round and couldn't get off it. I was tired.

"How's Stewart?" I changed the subject to his one-eyed cat he rescued in the recent months.

"He misses you," he said.

I shook my head and closed my eyes in defeat.

"Your mom's dog, Colton, I think his name is, or they call him Colt? He's adorable," he said, changing the subject.

"My mom's what?" I said in disbelief.

"Your mom's new dog. He's a little brown chihuahua mix. He's a pudgy little dude, but as friendly as they come," Meiser chuckled.

"I didn't know my mom got a dog. How do you know my mom has a dog?"

"I still talk to your family," he said simply.

"What does that mean? And do not skirt the subject this time. This is my family I'm asking about, not yours," I said, feeling like smoke was coming out of my nostrils. Those jerks betrayed me for brown hair, big dark eyes, and a hot body. Okay, I guess I kind of got it.

"What? I think your family is a hoot. I text with your aunt, uncle, grandma, and mom now and again to see how they are doing and if they need anything. Your grandma texts me at least a few times a week. I didn't know that you didn't know. Your mom's been thinking about getting a dog for a few weeks. She's been looking," he said. "How do you not know this?"

"I don't know! How do *you* know it?!" I yelled.

Betsy came out from the back, "Everything okay out here?"

Tabitha's comment popped into my head all of a sudden, which was odd.

"We're fine. Betsy, are you and Teddy seeing

each other?" I asked.

"We're friends," her body stiffened, and her head jerked back in surprise. . .

"Guess that means they're dating," Meiser said under his breath.

"Be quiet, you!"

"Why?" she asked.

"Tabitha asked me if he's seeing anyone, and I told her I wasn't sure. I wanted to let you know," I said.

My cell rang, and I looked down to see that my grandma was calling.

"Huh, looks like Grandma is calling me. Wonder what she would have to say to me that she doesn't want you to know?"

"Hello? Are you sure you didn't mean to dial Meiser's number?" I asked in a snotty tone.

"Jolie, someone attacked your Aunt Fern. She's in the hospital."

Panic shot through me.

"On my way," I said, grabbing my stuff and running out the door. Meiser came with me.

Chapter Twelve

Meiser and I rushed into Pine Valley hospital, and he asked at the desk for Fern Tucker's room number. We took the elevator up.

"This is all my fault," I said, tearing up.

"How is this your fault?"

"I keep getting involved in these things, and now someone in my family is paying for it," I said, putting my face in my hands.

Meiser grabbed me and hugged me. "We don't know what happened yet. It could have been a random crime."

"Thanks for coming with me." I looked up at him.

"Of course, I'll always be here for you," he said.

We headed to Aunt Fern's room, only to find a crowd of people pouring out of the room into the hallway while a frantic-looking young nurse tried to get their attention.

"Listen, you all can't be here. Most of you need to go to the waiting room, then two at a time can come and visit," she said.

No one but me was listening to her. I shoved

past the Martinez family and part of my family to get to Aunt Fern's side.

"What happened?" I took a breath when I saw she was okay.

"Some little punk with red-hair and freckles ran into me with his bike, and I fell off the curb. Everyone's making a big fuss out of nothing. That little jerk didn't even stop to see if I was okay," she said, shaking a fist in the air.

"Was it Tink?" I asked.

"What kind of name is that?" Aunt Fern asked. "The kid didn't smell that I could tell."

Meiser and I looked at each other and grinned. "It's a street nickname, I believe."

"Well, that's just dumb! Why would you give yourself that nickname? I don't know who that is," she said, reaching for the remote and turning it to *Cupcake Wars*. "Shhhhh, everyone shush, I want to watch my show."

"Oh, hey, Mom, you don't have Colt with you now?" I asked.

"He's at home. They won't let him in the hospital," she said as if nothing was going on.

"I want to babysit him. When can he stay the night with me?" Grandma Opal asked.

"I didn't even know I had a younger brother," I said angrily.

Grandma, Mom, Aunt Fern, and Uncle Wylie all looked at each other and then burst out laughing.

"She gets so cute when she gets angry," Aunt Fern said.

"I know, her face always gets blotchy red and her cheeks puff out," Grandma howled.

"Don't forget the hands-on hips and knees slightly bent," Meiser chimed in, laughing.

Oh, My Ever-loving Savior. This was it. This was truly it. Where is Tabitha when I needed her? If only she could see this, then she'd let everything slide and completely understand why I'm a whack job. I-I-I don't even know how to react to this. I was standing, twitching silently.

"Oh my gosh, now she's mentally losing it. She's wondering how to react," Ava's voice pealed.

I looked at her disbelievingly.

"You all need to give the child a break. No wonder she needs the therapy," Mrs. Martinez said.

"Don't butt your nose into my kid's personal business," my mom spat out.

"Patty, you've been a bit of a hot-head. I see where Jolie gets it," Lolly said.

"Don't think because you're an adult, I won't turn you over my knee Mrs-I'm-too-good-to-visit," my grandma said to Lolly.

"You will not lay a hand on my wife," Theo said.

"Shut up, you idiot," Thiago, Ava's father said to his son-in-law. "You're ready to defend her now that you've royally screwed up your marriage."

"Papa, don't!" Lolly cried.

Ava and I looked at each other. Tears were welling up in both our eyes. She came and grabbed me and headed out just in time as the young nurse had security moving to Aunt Fern's room.

We went back to my cottage, and Bobbi Jo jumped on the island in the kitchen and reached a paw out to Ava.

"Hey girl," she said, rubbing my calico bobtailed

beauty.

"Aw, you two are getting along today?" I asked, surprised. The two had a long history of feuding.

"I think she knows I've had it with both our families, and she feels sorry for me. It won't last." Ava head-butted Bobbi Jo.

"It's too much, right? It's not just me. I'm not crazy, am I? They are all out of control?"

"Um, yes, they are all nutjobs! I need my family to go to another country, like stat!" She exclaimed.

"What about me? Mine live here. They won't leave," I said in desperation.

"Your problem, not mine," she grinned.

"I hate you," I said.

"Hate you more," she stuck her tongue out at me.

"Let's talk about something else and add to our I Spy list," I said, grabbing the laptop.

"I still think Nestle is somehow involved in all this," Ava said.

"That's because you can't stand him," I said.

"And you can?"

"No, and I agree with you."

"I signed up for some online PI courses," Ava said. "I'm going to start with some criminal justice courses."

"Wow, you are serious about this!"

"Yeah, I never thought I was one for college, and I love what we do. No way will I ever give that up. But I don't know, the last year, I've really enjoyed trying to figure out the things that have been happening. It's something different. I like that we do it together, too."

"I hate to admit it, but there is an adrenaline rush that comes with it. I haven't shared that in my therapy sessions. Tabitha is trying to get me to explain why I keep putting myself in danger. I'm so happy you get it. It's hard to explain, though."

"Yeah, it's like, I get why most people wouldn't understand it. I wouldn't have understood it two years ago," Ava said.

"Me neither," I said.

"You should get a license, too," she said, clapping her hands together.

"I'll let you start the classes first, and then I'll decide," I said, not thinking I could take on anything new.

"Maybe it's better for me because my family is gone and I have more time on my hands," she said.

"Now you sound like your channeling Tabitha."

"Yeah, well, you've been sharing so much about your sessions, how can that not spill over to me," Ava grinned.

"Right? And your PI training will end up spilling over to me, too!"

"What was Meiser doing at the hospital with you?" Ava asked.

"Uh, another topic Tabitha keeps dredging up. I honestly don't mean to be rude here, but I don't know. The entire situation with him, Keith--and now Tabitha is relating it all to my bio father and how I grew up with trust issues--is making me feel like I'm going crazy. I want to be with Meiser. He wants to be with me. But something keeps telling me this isn't the right time."

"Why not?"

"I can't put my finger on it. He's not telling me

everything. I just can't. I won't be with someone who can't be honest with me," I said.

"I get that," Ava said.

"Thank you!"

"I could be a therapist, too," Ava said.

"You could do it all." I smiled.

She nodded in agreement.

"Okay, PI Martinez, what shall we add to our I Spy Slides today?"

"I like the sound of that," Ava said.

"Me, too."

"We need to write in our notes that Nestle didn't follow me but met Tink at the hospital the night I was attacked," I said.

"Right, but he could have known and sent the intruder or paid someone to do it for all we know," Ava said, typing away.

"Or for all we know, Nestle was paid off and paid someone else off," I said.

"This is getting too complicated."

"Go to Tink's picture," I said.

"Yeah, let's question whether he had anything to do with Fernie," Ava said, typing it in under the notes.

"Right, we've got Nestle, the stranger who was arguing with Meiser, and Tink all connected somehow," I said.

"And Meiser, we need to add his picture too," she said, searching for a picture of him.

"What? Why would you say that?"

"I'm not saying he's involved, but he's connected to these people in some way," Ava said.

I didn't like seeing his picture mixed in with possible criminals, but I had mentioned it earlier when we started all of this—he has been talking to that strange man.

"Type in 'gentrification.' That was the topic Pria kept bringing up. It's related to urban sprawl, and that was an issue that Nestle was messed up in last summer," I said.

"I'm going to make a different slide for it," Ava said.

"She said something about getting them to use the money for rec centers instead of condos," I said.

Ava typed that in.

"Maybe we should take a quick trip to that area of town and see if condos are going up and how much they are asking for them," I said.

"Sounds like a plan," Ava said, grabbing her purse.

We drove through the area of the city where the rec center was and saw that an art gallery had recently been built. It was the nicest building on the block with the fanciest sign.

"I'm going to assume that is the start of change in this neighborhood," I said, pointing.

Ava pulled over and we walked inside. It was beautiful. There was sleek marble round table tops spread around the large room with nude sculptures on some of the tables to the left of the room and wood-carved animals on the right side. Huge abstract paintings in bright colors covered large canvases on the walls. A mini-bar sat in a corner with a few sleek stools, and there was vibrant-colored mesh ceiling art that hung above the bar.

Everything had a price tag that was what Ava and I made together in a year.

"Hi, ladies, interested in our exhibit?" A lanky woman in all black with long, black, straight, shiny hair said. She reached out a well-manicured hand to shake mine.

"Hello, this place is beautiful," I said. "I can't help but notice it's in a rough part of town, though. Doesn't that affect your business and clientele?"

"Oh, well, this neighborhood will be changing soon. No need to be afraid, we have security inside and out twenty-four-seven, ladies." She pointed to two beefy uniformed men with scowls on their faces. I noticed they were armed, too.

"Wow, that has to be pricey," Ava said.

Miss Lanky gave Ava an up and down distasteful look and directed her attention toward me. This better not be a racial thing. Because if it was, I would...

"The mayor of Tri-City himself is very invested in this neighborhood," she said to me.

"Mayor Cardinal, of course," I said, looking at Ava. "Do you know if they plan to build any condos or houses in the area?"

"Why, are you looking to buy?" She again directed her question to me.

"Yes, my girlfriend and I are ready to make the move to the city. We're looking to be in a neighborhood that is up and coming. Ava here is a Latino goddess. She does the most wonderful oil paintings you've ever seen. In Santo Domingo, she is the most famous artist they have," I said drawing out several words, with my nose in the air and putting my arm around Ava. The only thing that would have made my speech perfect was if I added

D-A-R-L-I-N-G at the end of the statement.

Ava grinned at me.

"*Oh,* I didn't *realize,*" Lanky-Jerk-Face said walking back her privileged tone and showing Ava some respect. "Well, we have some oil paintings in the back. I'd love for you to look at them–Miss?"

"Martinez, darling," Ava extended her hand daintily which made me almost choke trying not to laugh. Of course, she would add darling!

"Of course, Miss Martinez, please follow me."

As Ava headed to the back, I walked past Bruiser and Goliath and smiled meekly at them giving them a single pinky-finger wave.

I headed out to the street, looking up and down. There were a bunch of run-down buildings just like the street that led to the Mayor's house. I noticed a kid with tattered clothes sitting in a corner.

"Hey there, you live around here?" I asked.

"Yeah, you could say that lady," he said, chomping on something.

"Do you know if they are building condos somewhere on this street?" I asked.

He shook his head north, "See that big brown, crumbling brick building?"

"Yeah," I said.

"They're going to tear it down and build. Lots of my friends live there."

I looked around and saw a burger joint across the street. I was thinking about running over and buying the kid a meal when Bruiser came barreling out of the art building.

"I told yer before, you little punk, don't be buzzin' around this building. And leave the patrons alone!" he barked, towering over the kid.

The poor kid shook. "Sorry, mister, she came up to me," he said, glaring at me.

Ava came stomping out of the building next. She ran up and put her weight into a tackle against Bruiser's back knocking him slightly forward. The man was a tank.

"Whoa, awesome!" The kid yelled jumping up and grinning a yellow smile.

"You stupid—" the guard started.

The door swung open and Lanky strode out on her towering heels. "Tiny, please, come inside. These two women are intruders. There is no famous artist called Ava Martinez. She couldn't even tell a Gerson from a Giatto."

"I *love* gelato, lady," Ava smirked.

"Hey, kid, let's go get some burgers, fries, and shakes," Ava said, heading across the street.

"Really, lady?"

"Yep, it's on her," she pointed at me.

The kid followed along.

Once we finished devouring our fattening lunch, the kid took off with a bag of food that we bought him.

We stood outside the fast-food joint, and I showed Ava where the kid said they were building the condos. Except she wasn't looking. She was looking at a piece of paper taped to the window of the burger place.

"Hey, what are you looking at?"

"Look, they have a self-defense course being offered at the rec center." She looked at her watch.

"It's getting ready to start. Let's go!" She grabbed

my arm dragging me toward it.

We got there right as they were starting.

"Welcome, ladies! Let's make room for two more," a man in a pair of sweats and tee said.

I felt like I was going to vomit up my lunch after running down the road to get here.

The man began the session, showing us several ways to protect ourselves from assailants. It was very informative. Then, he had us pair up.

Ava wanted me to be the assailant.

"I don't want to get beat down," I said. "You're bigger than me–you be the assailant."

"That is size discrimination, chica!"

"Problem, ladies?"

It seemed we were making a scene. Shocker.

"Sorry," I said, obediently taking my stance as the assailant behind Ava.

I had come up from behind and wrapped my arms around her arms. Ava then was supposed to pretend to pull up her right foot and stomp on my foot causing me to bend forward, which would loosen my grip on her, giving her the opportunity to elbow me in the groin, then swing her hand back and hit me in the face.

Instead, she got a little too amped up and jabbed me directly in the stomach. With a heave, I barfed up my lunch onto her back. The entire class sucked in a collective breath of horror, including the instructor. And here I thought we had made a scene earlier.

Ava started yelling obscenities.

I held up one hand to my mouth and another to the crowd in apology. I hobbled toward the bathroom, still bent over from the gut-strike, forcibly towing my puke-covered friend with me. Once the door closed, I glared at her.

"Why did you do that?" I yelled.

"Me? You are *not* yelling at me right now as I stand here with your lunch regurgitated all over my favorite sweatshirt. Eck! This better not be in my hair!" She tried to see the back of her hair in the mirror. She grimaced and started pulling the sweatshirt off her head.

"Are you going to walk around with no clothes on?" I asked as she began tugging.

"Yeah, I'm going to go completely naked, Jolie. No, I have a tank top on underneath. Thank goodness! I guess I need to always wear one in case you decide to vomit on me." She carefully peeled off the sweatshirt and looked around, then shrugged her shoulders and threw it in the trash can.

"Whoa, once again, YOU were the one who wanted to come here. YOU were the one who drug me here running after I filled up on lunch, then YOU decided to elbow me really hard in the gut," I said.

"So, this is all my fault," Ava said, throwing her hands up in disbelief.

Again, my brain went into slow-mo. "YES!" I screamed.

A woman from the class came running in. "Hi, ladies. Um, Paul, the instructor, wanted me to check in on you. He asked that I give you both the pamphlets that go along with the course."

She began walking out of the bathroom and held the door open then turned around and said, "Also, he asked that you not come back."

She then ran out of the door.

"Well, that's rude," Ava said.

"Not really," I said.

"Whatever, we're now officially self-defense pros and it's one more step toward me being a PI. I say we refer to ourselves as the Kick Ass Sistas!"

Oh yeah, that works.

Chapter Thirteen

It had been a week since Thanksgiving, and I felt more confused than ever as to who was behind Pria's murder and who had planned the murder of Steve Smalls.

I had just finished prepping for lunch, and we were in that after breakfast—pre-lunch lull. I made a cup of tea and headed out front to flip through a magazine and take a break. I stood still holding the magazine in one hand and tea in the other when I saw Meiser sitting at a table. He grinned and pushed out a chair for me to join him.

Ava was sitting at the counter working on the schedule and paying some bills. She gave me a look as I headed his way.

"Sorry to barge in on you. I was hoping you'd have time to talk." He wrapped his hand around the warm coffee cup, blowing on it before carefully sipping.

I just stared at him. I'm not sure for how long. I wanted to say something—be friendly—but I was also tired of the same song and dance. I set my magazine down and sipped my tea.

"His name is Marty." Meiser shifted in his seat.

"Who?"

"The strange man you asked me about earlier. His name is Marty. He's my brother," he said with a flat tone and his eyes dead-locked onto mine.

I took a couple of minutes to digest this information. Wow, Meiser had a brother. Mick and Marty. Cute. Meiser was opening up to me and trusting me. Nice. Meiser was still holding back. Not cool.

"Aren't you going to speak?" He frowned.

"You have a brother," I said nonchalantly.

"I have two brothers and a sister."

"Wow, okay then," I said sipping more tea. I had to digest all this.

"Obviously, I don't get along with my family. I am the complete opposite of all of them. There is a long history of..." he trailed off looking out the window.

I saw his jaw clench several times. I could tell he was reaching for the right words; he seemed afraid to tell the story.

I reached across the table and put my hand over his, coaxing him. "Go on, I can handle whatever it is you need to tell me."

Meiser lifted his eyes to mine, took a deep breath, and said, "The Italian mob."

He exhaled loudly, nervously running his hand through his hair. The Meiser I had come to know over the last year was cool, coy, and calm. His demeanor had changed while talking about his family to a man in angst and conflict.

"It doesn't even sound real when I say it out loud to you. It's like a bad nightmare that I can't wake up from."

And here I thought I had to adjust to the name change and the two brothers and one sister news. My mind was jumping all over the place, and I swallowed my tea down the wrong pipe and began choking obnoxiously. I couldn't see my face, but I assumed my expression was similar to when I'm stuffing myself at a meal—red face and bulging eyes.

Meiser leapt up and paced next to table. I don't think he knew whether to perform the Heimlich or bail. Ava rushed over with a glass of water as I grasped at a breath, gained control, and took a swig of water.

"Thanks." I looked up at her in relief.

"You better not be upsetting her," Ava stood hands on hips.

"Ava, thanks for the water. I need to finish this conversation in private," I said, stone-faced, a look she doesn't often get from me.

She hesitated, thought better of whatever was about to come out of her mouth, and turned back to continue her work.

"So, that's why you had your name legally changed?"

"Yes, that's why. Listen, it's a long, sordid story with a lot of history."

"I'd like to hear it."

"My family's connections are to the Sicilian mafia, and it dates back to the mid-nineteenth century. My great-great-grandfather got in a lot of trouble in Italy because he was part of the *mafie*."

"What's that?"

"The *mafie* were private smaller-scaled armies that extorted protection money from landowners," he paused and drank the rest of his coffee.

I reached across the table, grabbed his cup, and put a finger up for him to wait while I refilled his coffee. Extorting protection money from landowners. I needed to talk to Ava about this so we could look into the selling of property last summer.

"Sorry, this was the bottom of the pot. I put on a fresh brew," I said, sliding the cup over to him.

"No worries," he took a gulp and continued, "so believe it or not, many of the Sicilian mafia relocated to Ohio."

"Why Ohio?" I felt my entire face scrunch inward in confusion.

"Exactly right," he pointed at me.

"Ah, no one would expect Ohio," I said, catching on.

"Right, many went to Canada as well."

"Okaaay." I drug out the word and raised an eyebrow.

"Just listen for a minute. The mafia was strong and in control for much of the nineteenth century. It began to weaken in the twentieth century. During this time, those members that were arrested were not honoring the *omertã*, and that led to more arrests. This was when my family moved to Ohio to be more incognito."

"And *omertã* just means 'not honoring a code'?"

"In the early days, the men in the mafia wouldn't speak to anyone in law enforcement or the government or anyone to do with the law—it was their code of honor. So yeah, my brothers and sister and I grew up in this crazy world. As little kids, we didn't really know what was going on. I'm the third oldest. My dad wasn't opposed to taking the belt to us. My brothers readily obeyed."

"Let me guess–you didn't?"

"Not at all. It wasn't the path I wanted for myself. I paid for that, but once I turned seventeen, I ran off to take care of myself. At eighteen, I legally changed my name and basically started a new life for myself."

"So, you haven't seen or spoken to your family since you were seventeen?" I couldn't wrap my head around that.

"My sister, Maria, and I write letters to each other. It's old-fashioned, but I insisted because I didn't want my family to have my contact information. I went as far as putting gloves on when I wrote and sent it, so there were no fingerprints so no one could trace where I was."

"Wow, that's intense," I felt my body lean forward. "So, you're all M's."

"Yeah, my mama and papa are both M's too. It's confusing."

"So, how did your brother find you?" I asked

"He hired a PI when he heard I had MS. He won't tell me how he heard. I'm still working on that, but I believe it was Nestle."

"Nestle's involved in the mob?" I sat bolt upright.

"Like I said, it's a long, sordid story. It would take a whole other day to get into all that. Point is my brother knows about the MS, my new name, and he knows about you. I do not want you involved in this."

"Didn't you have some good times with your siblings as kids despite the family business? Are you positive all your siblings are involved?"

"Of course, we had fun as kids. Actually, I had a

wonderful childhood up until I found out the truth. My brother you saw me with, Marty, has always had this weird whistle that comes out of his nose when he gets worked up. As kids, we all tried to get him worked up to hear it. He'd get so mad at us." He laughed with a far-off look.

Oh crap, I felt heartstrings pulling for him. As much as my family made me want to run away to another country, all I know is a life with them. It had to be horrible finding out everything you thought was real wasn't, then watching your siblings begin to turn into what you hate. My mind was going a million miles an hour. I was thrilled he opened up to me—trusted me enough to do so. It hurt me that his brother cared enough to find him, and Mick was trying to find reasons to avoid him.

"Sorry to interrupt," Ava said, huffing heavily and leaning on the table.

I gave her an incredulous stare and slowly looked at the little length from the counter to our table, thinking she must be out of shape. The next thing she said made her hysteria understandable.

"I just got off the phone with Keith. He told me that both Nestle and Tink had an alibi when Smalls was killed," she panted.

"He should not be sharing that information," Meiser scowled.

"He didn't share it, nosey," Ava crossed her arms and glared down at him.

"Okay, I've tried to be nice, but how exactly am I the nosey one? I'm sitting here, minding my own business having a private conversation with Jolie, and you come barreling between us spilling your guts. You explain to me how that makes me nosey?" Meiser had shifted in his seat leaning toward Ava giving her an I-dare-you-to-come-back-at-me look.

Uh-oh, I did not like the way her entire body just tightened in one fell swoop.

Ava had not been friendly with Meiser at all since the lies this past summer. She was not good at faking how she felt or hiding what she thought.

Ava was seething. "Like I said before, he did not share it, nosey. He and I were on the phone making plans for a flag football game..." she turned her head to look at me mumbling under her breath *not that it's any of his business.*

I'm positive Meiser heard her.

"He was on a break at work. I heard it come over his walkie-talkie," Ava gave him a look that said he was the most incompetent person in the entire world.

"Radio," Meiser said flatly.

"Excuse me?" Ava countered.

"It's called a radio, not a walkie-talkie. We are not five-year-olds playing cops and robbers," Meiser pretended to say this under his breath quickly before taking a drink of his coffee.

"Oh, if you got something to say, then you just say it, my friend," Ava's rigid posture transformed into a hula-hoop-dance-like motion, with her finger moving back and forth toward his face.

Meiser sat calmly, grinned, and said, "What? I'm just taking a page from your script. Seems like you were the one being nosey, not me."

I jumped out of my seat and threw the weight of my body into Ava, who was ready to pounce on Meiser. "Whoa, okay, you two, both of you back to your corners. The bell has rung." I put a straight arm out between them.

Meiser stood up, towering over Ava.

"What are you going to do, punch her?" I started to get defensive.

"When you were *talking* to Keith, did you catch their alibis?" Meiser asked, brushing past us to grab some fresh coffee.

I noticed the others had come in for their shift. I had gotten so lost in Meiser's life that I had lost all track of time.

"Both of them were in Tri-City with Tink's family," Ava said, giving me a look that read We-need-to-add-this-to-our-I-Spy-Slides.

We can nearly read each other's minds most of the time.

"Wait, I swore Pria or Tink—someone told me he was new to the group. I don't know if I assumed he wasn't close to his family or that he was on the street. That seems odd. Also, Nestle and him again? Keith said they were meeting at the hospital the night of my attack." My mind was racing again.

"Can it," Meiser said, looking from me to Ava.

"What?"

"Stop playing detective. That's my job," he said, reaching for his trench coat. How appropes.

Meiser was reaching for his wallet when Ava said to me, "It looks like our families made amends after the hospital war they raged. My parents are still leaving on Sunday evening. Your family made arrangements to book the Community Center for early morning/afternoon so the village can have that Thanksgiving dinner after all."

"Seems too soon," I said, trailing off.

"Nah, it's a way to move on from all this," Meiser said, putting a twenty on the table.

"Seriously? How much is your annual salary? You did this with Betsy the other day—now you had coffee and a twenty?" I asked, shaking my head.

"Hey, if the man wants to leave a twenty, let him leave a twenty," Ava grabbed it and shoved it down her bra. "I guess you're invited too."

Meiser laughed, "Thanks—don't get overly excited. You really know how to make a guy feel welcome."

She rolled her eyes.

"You should invite your brother, Marty, too. Maybe there's something of your relationship to salvage?" I said, hopefully.

"Actually, he just texted me and wants me to meet him by the library. Maybe I'll ask," he said.

"I thought you didn't want him to know your number?"

"I gave it to him a few days ago." He reached down and pecked me on the cheek and headed out the door with a curt salute in Ava's direction.

Ava did a low whistle, "Whoa, so you two are back together."

"Why would you say that?"

"You two are making out on the sidewalk, having hot beverages and intense truth-time here, and now he's pecking you on the cheek as he leaves like you are married."

"That is ridiculous, we are just..."

Ava enjoyed getting me worked up, and she whistled again as I spun around to head to the back to grab my tote, but I stopped suddenly and slowly spun around on my heels.

"What's wrong?" Ava leaned in, grabbing my arm.

"The whistle," I said, pointing at the door.

"Huh? I know you can't whistle. I like to tease you." Ava laughed.

"No, the whistle. You said someone whistled at you when you were near Nestle and Mick's brother," I said.

"Yeah, I am hot, so..."

"My attacker had a whistle Ava—when he breathed, I heard a whistling sound. Meiser just said—Oh God!" I leaned back into nothing and almost fell over, but Ava grabbed me.

"What's going on, Jolie. Use your words. You're scaring me."

"His brother, Marty, he just told me he had a funny whistle when he got worked up as a kid! He's on his way to meet him now! I have to go—give me your phone," I said, reaching for her pocket where I saw the lump of her phone as tears welled up in my eyes.

Ava grabbed it and threw it at me, then yelled at Magda to get ahold of either the chief or Keith and have them get to the library ASAP—she went sprinting out the door behind me.

I'm not a runner, neither is Ava, but I was moving fast. Ava had fallen behind, and then I didn't see her.

I got to the front of the library and didn't see Meiser. I ran inside and asked at the front desk if he had come in recently. The girl at the desk told me she hadn't seen him. I headed back outside and crossed the street to go near the hospital. Keith had said Nestle met Tink in the parking garage ground floor. I headed there.

Standing in place in the middle of the garage, I slowly swung my body around, looking for anyone talking near vehicles. My heart felt like it was pounding through my chest. What if I couldn't find them? Surely his brother wouldn't kill him. We didn't have time to try to see if we could make it or not. I willed my mind to focus. I noticed a blur of movement near the elevators and moved closer. There was an opening and a cement wall that led to the stairs. I heard voices as I moved to hide behind the wall.

"Marty, you don't want to do this, man. I thought we were going to try and work through things," Meiser said. I peeked around and could see he had his hands up defensively.

"Nah, too late for that big-shot Detective. You brought shame to our family name."

"I don't share the family name anymore. How could I bring shame to it?"

"That's the point—who disowns their own family? Papa says the MS is your punishment for how you have treated us." Marty's voice was flat.

"Hey man, why Pria?" Meiser asked.

"Who?"

"Are you kidding me? You've turned into a monster! The girl you had Smalls kill—why did that have to happen?" Meiser demanded.

"Smalls was a street rat who worked for me. She was a street rat too. The money she stole from him is money he owed me," Marty sneered.

"She didn't know that, Marty. She was a kid trying to survive for crying out loud!"

"Yeah, well, we are all just trying to survive. There are codes we live by. War is war."

"War? What? Yes, for soldiers—war is war—different rules. These streets," I peeked and could see Meiser moving his hands around, "not war."

"Isn't it?" Marty's nose began to whistle, and I assumed from his tone that a sinister grin began to form across his lips. "My buddy tells me your lady friend thinks she's some sort of detective, rooting around at crime scenes."

I saw a flicker of hate in Meiser's eyes and feared he would attack his brother regardless of weapons he held. I saw Marty move toward Meiser and they were near the wall adjacent to me. I slowly and quietly leaned around the wall to see more, when I saw the shine of the blade moving toward Meiser.

I had no thoughts, just action. I leaped at Marty and jumped on his back, feeling the knife knick my forearm that I had wrapped around his neck. I saw Meiser from the corner of my eye begin leaning to grab his brother, but Marty flipped me over his shoulder and stood me up quickly positioning the knife at my jugular.

Meiser didn't move a muscle. "Hey man, come on, this is between you and me."

"Nah, looks like your new and improved lifestyle has rubbed off on your little *la donna*," he said, rubbing the blade of the knife up and down my neck while holding my chin up with his other hand. "One could argue you may have been better off to stick with your *famiglia*."

Meiser looked into my eyes. He looked terrified.

I used my eyes to look at a can on the ground, hoping he could read my mind like Ava could. I wanted him to make a noise to district Marty.

On cue, he looked down at the can, looked up at me, squishing his eyebrows together, and kicked the can.

Marty took one second to loosen his grip while his mind was distracted by the noise. I used that second to raise my foot and stomp as hard as I could on his foot, which caused the knife to cut into my throat, but then Marty's body obediently doubled over, giving me the opportunity free my arm to take aim at his crotch with my elbow. Again, his body followed self-defense protocol, and he leaned over, dropping the knife and allowing me to take my fist and bring it back to knock him in his face where he fell to the ground.

"That was—" BEEP-BEEP—a horn honked trying to get out of the garage, "—ing awesome," Ava had used an expletive that I never heard her use before. She must have come up as everything was going down. She was limping and holding onto the wall.

Meiser had kicked the knife to the side, and we heard sirens racing toward us. As the sirens pulled into the garage, I saw Meiser bend to the ground and whisper something into Marty's ear, then get up, grin down at his brother, and proceed to kick him hard in the side before Teddy and Keith came to the scene.

Keith grabbed Marty and cuffed him while reading him his Miranda rights.

Meiser walked over to me, "Ava was right. That was awesome."

"Ah, it was nothing. We took a self-defense course, and that was the one single move I learned," I said feeling my face flush.

"You saved yourself, and you saved my life," he said, reaching down for my hand.

"You two need to come with me so I can get your statements," Teddy said, interrupting the moment.

Keith looked at Meiser, and I then shoved Marty into the police car.

Marty looked at Meiser from the window as they drove away and spit at the window.

Gross!

Chapter Fourteen

It was early Sunday afternoon, and I actually was in the holiday mood! People in the village decided to shut down many of the shops and restaurants so we could all be together at the Community Center. We all started the day by taking a moment of silence for Pria. The teens had brought a large bouquet of fall flowers and made a heart out of construction paper that they glued to the front that read, "R.I.P. Pria—you will be missed. We all love and appreciate you."

We ordered pizzas and paid by credit card over the phone (the entire village chipped in) and had the teens pick them up from the city and bring them in. Betsy brought desserts, and many of us brought some snacks and appetizers.

The mayor showed the pull he had and had outdone himself by hiring a team to come into the Community Center and redecorate the auditorium and the kitchen. Rather than old cafeteria tables, he sprung for the round mobile bench tables, which felt cozier and homier. Our local florist in the village had beautiful autumn arrangements on each table, and Delilah had worked with some of the kids in town to create fun autumn wreaths as well as

Hanukah-themed wreaths, Christmas wreaths, and other-religious-related holiday wreaths. Our village had always prided ourselves on having one place of worship that shared the pulpit between multiple faiths.

The kitchen had long needed new appliances, and there were all new stainless-steel stoves with gas burners and grilled tops, microwaves, a new freezer—which I was especially happy to see, and more. I had no idea how the man could afford to make this happen. It all had to be expensive to begin with, but to do all this in such a short amount of time had to cost extra.

Ava and I were at a table with some of the teens when the Martinez and Tucker family walked up behind us.

"Good lord, that is creepy," Ava said, looking over her shoulder in horror.

"Real nice you think your family is creepy," Sophia said.

Theo and Lolly were holding hands. Ava told me they had decided to get couples counseling when they returned to Santo Domingo, and were committed to working through their issues.

"We need to be heading out, my *querido niño*," Thiago said to Ava. He's always called her "my dear child," similar to my mom calling me "Sunshine" my whole life.

Ava and I stood up to hug everyone.

"Not yet, sit back down, you two," my grandma scolded us.

Ava and I nervously glanced at each other and immediately sat back down.

My mom grabbed her phone and scrolled

through her photos. There were several close-ups of individual Polaroids–pictures of pictures. She tapped one to enlarge it and tilted the screen toward us, showing an image of us as five-year-olds with our kitchen set up in the playroom and the dolls that had the cast iron skillet key-chain homemade necklaces that Ava made.

"Yep, that's us as little tots," I said, not understanding where this was going. I didn't much like to be reminded of that time. Ava, on the other hand, was beside herself cooing and ahhing at how cute we were and pointing at the necklaces–grinning, asking if I remembered.

"Of course, I do. You were designing Cast Iron Creations way back in the day." I tried to sound excited but felt my eyes drift to the window as I remembered what happened after that nap. After the phone call. My bio dad's voice, wailing over the phone line.

I woke up feeling like nothing had happened—like it was all a bad dream. I rubbed my eyes and saw that Ava was still sawing logs, so I got up and wandered toward the kitchen.

I heard my mom talking to someone, but I didn't know who. "No, Ed, no! She can't know. He's already messing with her head. He's manipulating her and trying to manipulate me, and I'm not going to let it happen."

"Patty, he tried to take his life. I don't think that is a manipulative game," this Ed guy said.

"She's too young. I'm not telling her. Plus, the one time she tells him how she really feels about him standing her up, and he does this. It's sick."

I headed back to the bedroom and slid by Ava, who was still asleep. I had never told anyone what

I had heard. I was terrified to say or do the wrong thing around my dad from that day on.

"Earth to Jolie!" Ava was waving a hand in front of my face.

"Whoa, sorry everyone--that picture took me back in time." I plastered on a fake smile.

"Before we go, both families wanted to do something nice for you girls to show you how proud we are of you," Grandma Opal said. She looked over to my mom and Sophia, who each took a cute, small, pink-hearted wrapped box out from behind their backs and presented them to us.

Ava and I grinned broadly at one another, grabbed the boxes, and tore into what was beautiful wrapping. Inside the boxes were matching cast-iron locket necklaces.

"Whoa!"

"Wow!" We both said in unison.

"Your girlfriend helped us design them from the picture of what you made, Ava," Sophia said as she put her arm around Delilah.

Ava and I exchanged a knowing look.

"These are the perfect gifts!" I reached out to hug everyone involved.

Ava followed my lead doing the same, and then we saw her family out the door.

"I miss them already." Ava looked at me with tears in her eyes.

"We are both crazy," I said, patting her on the back.

"That is a statement I can agree with." Meiser sauntered up to us.

"My cue to leave! But first–" Ava unexpectedly

reached out to hug him. "Happy late Thanksgiving."

Meiser timidly reached around Ava to hug her while side-eyeing me.

"Yowsa, was that real, or should I be watching my back?" he stage-whispered.

"I'd not worry today but be cautious in the future." I smiled.

Meiser pointed to the locket I was holding in my hand. "I admit to being nosey. I was at the next table and heard what your families did for you both. That was nice." He reached for the locket.

"Yeah, they're not all bad. I guess." I did the aw-shucks shuffle while batting my eyelashes.

"Want me to put it on you?" He reached for the locket.

I turned around and took both hands to lift the shoulder-length blonde curls off my neck. Meiser reached around to attach the latch, and I felt his breath on my ear. His hand grazed the back of my neck softly—a tingle ran up and down my body and I shivered.

"Are you cold?" He unbuttoned his blazer.

"No, I'm fine—just a momentary chill." I looked away, but not before I caught the hunger in his eye and the seductive smile playing on his lips.

"Hey, I wanted to apologize to you." He put an arm around my waist and led me outside where it was quieter.

"For what?"

He proceeded to take his blazer off and put it around my shoulders anyway, blocking the chill in the air. I looked up and smiled at him.

"I think you were right in what you said earlier."

"Wow, that's a first!" I declared. "What was I right about?" I was ready to hear him say I was wrong about us not being ready for a relationship, but I was right in that we both needed to do some work on ourselves due to family issues. It felt like we could finally be on the same page. I never thought I'd get to this place.

"I think you are right to take the time you need. As much as I don't want to say this, maybe we both should move on. I was wrong to believe I could get away from my family and they wouldn't find me. I've put you in danger. I think it's best that we both move on from each other." His face was a mask of pain, and his eyes seemed to be reaching for something I wasn't able to give him after that speech.

I stood like a statue, then what felt like slow-motion, I removed the blazer from my shoulders and handed it to him. I took in a deep breath, looked him the eye, smiled politely, and said, "I'm so sorry about your brother being arrested for putting the hit on Pria and Smalls. I hope you don't feel it necessary to leave town. I believe we could remain friends."

"Friends would be nice." He grabbed the blazer. He leaned in to kiss me but stopped himself. He squared his shoulders. "Take care, Jolie, I'm sure I'll see you around town."

My brain felt frozen in time, but my body went through the motions of moving back into the auditorium, eating pizza, chatting with those around me as if nothing at all was wrong. I looked around and saw the people of the village interacting with the teens of the city—everyone was smiling, laughing, and swapping stories. Delilah, Ava, Lydia, and Betsy were all huddled up with me and chitchatting as I grinned and nodded at what sounded like the Charlie Brown teacher in my head.

I heard several people gasp, and some went moving to the door. I looked over and saw my mom had brought her new puppy, Colt, over. I moved outside to see and meet the little guy.

"Well, you've always wanted a brother or sister, Jolie—meet your new little brother Colt," Ava said, bending next to him as he jumped in her face licking her cheek.

Colt was goldish-beige, pudgy little guy with white under his chin on his neck. He looked like a mix between a chihuahua and a Jack Russell terrier. He had the puppy black snout and dark eyes—funny, he looked right into my eyes and seemed to sense the pain I felt. He sat down on his back legs and raised two front paws at me whining.

I bent down and picked him up in my arms. "Hi, guy, how are you? I'm your sissy!"

Colt reached out to my face and gave me a big kiss making me giggle, and I noticed the pain that was in his eyes turned to humor at my laughter. I always thought a lot of people really underestimated the power of a companion who would love them unconditionally. Dr. Libby would agree with me that many animals understand human emotions—sometimes better than we understand it ourselves. This little guy seemed to understand me.

My mom was smiling ear to ear as she reached for her new child. Colt knew who his mom was as he reached his paws toward her. She beamed with pride. Those two would be good for each other, and if anyone in this world deserved happiness, it was my mother. She wasn't perfect by far, but she had a heart of gold. That woman would take a bullet for me or readily cut a limb off for me. As much as she drove me nuts, I'd do the same for her or anyone in my family.

Much of the party had moved outside, and I saw Tink walk up to our family. He grinned and asked to pet Colt. I noticed him looking around closely at our entire family. The kid creeped me out a bit.

I looked over, and a couple with four teens came walking up to where Tink was petting Colt. The man's face had the same bone structure as Tink's. I noticed my mom's body tighten, then looked around and saw Aunt Fern, Uncle Wylie, and Grandma Opal's expressions of shock.

My mom ran to the man. "Eddie, I've missed you so much!"

Grandma Opal looked to have steam blowing out her ears. Her face was beet red; I noticed her hands were clenched tightly into fists, and her eyes were shooting darts at the man my mom was hugging. Aunt Fern looked the same.

"Hey, Sis, I'd like you to meet my wife and five kids," Eddie said to my mom.

My jaw dropped; my brain had a wrench thrown into it, and nothing was processing. I glanced over to Tink. His eyes were locked on me. My cousin?

Chapter Fifteen

Sunday 12/8/19

It's been a full week since chaos has wrecked my world.

When I was a kid—the times my bio dad decided to actually pick me up and take me for his day—which were few and far between—he preferred to ask me about "Mommy" and how she was doing and who she was seeing—never how I was doing. He'd tell me things like, "You know your family has big secrets that they like to keep from you." The first time he said it, I asked him what the secret was. "Can't tell you. That's why it's a secret." I never asked again. Honestly, I didn't believe him. When he would bring it up after that, I would just shrug. Over time, I became numb to him. Don't get me wrong, I knew better than to stand my ground for fear he'd hurt himself—I also worried he'd hurt mom or me. So, I learned to go with the flow. If he showed up, then I'd go, and I hated it. I'd just be a robot and answer his questions and try to be a good little girl.

As I got older, from time to time, I'd let it all build up inside me and then tell my bio dad I was *done again. At the age of eight, he and I were alone at his house together. We were watching TV in his basement, and he had asked several questions about my mom. How was she? Was she seeing anyone? Did she ever talk about him? Did she ever ask about him? Did I think she'd ever get back together with him? I was trying to watch a movie, and I snapped again. As soon as I did, I felt my muscles clench and my eyes widen. I remember he smiled at me. But it was a different smile. It reminded me of the old Joker cartoon character smile. Very sinister. He said he was going up to get more iced tea. I remember being relieved that he walked away. Finally, it was quiet, and I could just watch the movie.*

I finished the movie and realized he had never come back down. I remember rolling my eyes and thinking, "Now what?" and pulling myself off the couch, not wanting to have to seek him out. I drug myself upstairs to the kitchen—not there. Walked into the living room—not there. Walked the six steps up to the next floor where the bathroom was to the right. The door was shut and locked. I knocked lightly, nothing. I knocked a little louder and heard an odd gurgling sound. I pounded on the door and jerked at the doorknob. I ran out of the house and sprinted to the next-door neighbor, who I had never met. I pounded on the door, and a short, stout Latino man answered, looking confused. I pointed to my bio father's house, spilling out what I thought had happened. The stranger grabbed his cordless phone, dialed 9-1-1, and reported the incident, then threw the phone down and ran back to the house with me. I showed him where the bathroom was, and he began shoving at the door with his body. I stood still with arms hanging down, breathing heavily, while the

Hulk continued to thrash at the door. The stranger finally got the wooden door to give way; I ran up behind him and saw my bio dad lying on the tile of the bathroom with foam coming out of his mouth.

"Daddy loves you," he mumbled from the floor as sirens wailed.

I don't remember a lot after that. My family wouldn't allow me to see him for a long time. I felt a hatred toward him, but also worried about him constantly, and felt guilty. Mom took me to a therapist then, but I don't remember a lot about that time in my life. It all felt like I was going through the motions without really living. There was a physical and mental pain that I felt like I had to live with forever—while faking a normal life on the surface. I went to school, did my homework, did the family holiday things—some days and times were harder than others, and I'd get extremely moody and angry—I think anyone would after faking for so long while feeling so much pain. The muscles in my body turned into literal knots—my body locked up all the time. I was terrified something I'd say or do would cause someone to hurt themselves. I felt cursed.

There's my homework, Tabitha. I believe we could call that a breakthrough of sorts. I've not been able to think about all that for some time now.

Moving to today, I think Meiser wanting to move on is the main thing that brought all this back. My default mode is to retreat inside, go back to going through the motions. I was finally ready to put things behind me and try to have a real relationship with him, and now he doesn't want it.

Keith and I had that long-awaited talk, and that was another break-through for me. I told him the *truth—the full truth. I didn't try to hide anything, and although I couldn't help but have that fear that I'd cause him to hurt himself, I trudged forth. I told him my brain believes he is the right man for me because of our past together. He told me the truth, but I was honest in saying that I was angry with him for telling me the truth about Meiser and that I knew that wasn't fair. Then, I let him have it all— I told him that regardless of what my brain said, my heart wants Meiser. It killed me to see the pain in his eyes. He wasn't happy. He said it was okay, but I saw that pain turn to anger. He's avoided me since.*

So, here I am, alone, single, Meiser and I are being fake friends, Keith is avoiding me. Even though I'm still talking to my family, it's all weird after finding out about a secret uncle and his wife and FIVE kids. So, I'm back to going through the motions—my protective mode has set in. Here's my question for you, Tabitha: I've supposedly made this breakthrough of understanding where all this comes from—taking it back to all the family drama that shaped me—and yet, I'm right back to that eight-year-old self of putting walls up and going through the motions to protect myself. So, how is that progress? I still feel like I'm eating pavement.

Recipes

Dutch Cast Iron Cajun Turkey Recipe

Ingredients for Turkey

Purchase one 6 to 8-pound turkey, patted dry

Kosher salt and freshly ground black pepper to taste

1/2 cup Cajun Spice Mix (see below for ingredients to make your mix)

1 celery stalk, coarsely chopped

1 green bell pepper, coarsely chopped

1 medium onion, coarsely chopped

1/4 cup (or more) olive or vegetable oil

Ingredients for Cajun Spice Mix

5 tablespoons kosher salt

2 tablespoons cayenne pepper

2 tablespoons garlic powder

2 tablespoons sweet paprika

1 tablespoon dried oregano

1 tablespoon dried thyme

1 tablespoon freshly ground black pepper

1 tablespoon onion powder

Stir together.

NOTE: You can make the spice mix up to one month ahead. Store in an airtight container at room temperature.

Recipe Preparation

NOTE: If you'd like your turkey to have a crisp coat, then you can add a little oil to a large cast iron skillet and lay the turkey in the skillet once it's hot for 30 seconds moving turkey around to brown it before putting in Dutch Cast Iron Pot. You would do this after the turkey has been at room temperature for an hour.

Set a rack inside a large, heavy Dutch Cast Iron Pot. Season turkey lightly inside and out with salt and pepper, then with spice mix, massaging it into the skin. Transfer turkey, breast side down, to prepared pan and refrigerate, uncovered, overnight.

Remove turkey from refrigerator; let stand at room temperature for 1 hour.

Preheat oven to 375°. Mix celery, pepper, and onion in a medium bowl. Fill turkey cavity with vegetable mixture, scattering any remaining vegetables over bottom of roasting pan. Brush turkey with oil.

Roast turkey, basting occasionally, for 1 hour. Using paper towels, flip turkey. Continue roasting, basting occasionally, until an instant-read thermometer inserted into the thickest part of thigh registers 165°, 1–1 1/2 hours longer. Transfer to platter. Let rest for at least 20 minutes before carving.

Honey-Glazed Turkey with Lemon-Sage Gravy

Ingredients

1 package (3/4 ounce) fresh sage, leaves chopped (about 5 tablespoons)

1 tablespoon salt

1 tablespoon pure ground black pepper

1 tablespoon garlic powder

3 small lemons

1 fresh or frozen (thawed) turkey (6 to 8 pounds for a Dutch Cast Iron Pot)

1 celery rib, coarsely chopped

1 onion, quartered

1 cup 100% pure honey

3 cans (14.5 ounces each) less-sodium chicken broth

1/3 cup all-purpose flour

Recipe Preparation

NOTE: If you'd like your turkey to have a crisp coat, then you can add oil to a large cast-iron skillet and lay the turkey in the skillet once it's hot for 30 seconds moving turkey around before putting in Dutch Cast Iron Pot.

1. Adjust oven rack to lowest position. Preheat oven to 325°. Place roasting rack in Dutch Cast Iron Pot. In small bowl, combine 2 tablespoons sage, salt, pepper, and garlic powder. Cut 1 lemon into quarters.

2. Remove giblets, liver, and neck from turkey cavities; freeze or save for later use. Prepare turkey

as package directs; place turkey, breast side up, on rack in pan. Sprinkle inside cavity and outside of turkey with sage mixture. Place celery, onion, and lemon quarters inside the cavity. If not already secured, tie legs together with kitchen string; tuck wing tips under turkey to hold in place. Tent turkey loosely with aluminum foil; roast 1-1/2 hours.

3. Meanwhile, from remaining 2 lemons, grate 1 tablespoon peel and squeeze 3 tablespoons juice. In microwave-safe medium bowl, heat honey, lemon peel, and 1 tablespoon juice in microwave oven on high 30 seconds or until easy to blend; stir in 2 tablespoons sage. With brush, baste turkey with some honey mixture.

4. Pour 1 can (1-3/4 cups) broth into bottom of roasting pan. Tent turkey with foil; roast 2-1/2 to 3 hours longer, basting every 20 to 30 minutes with warmed honey mixture. (Pop up temperature indicator may not work properly and stick with honey basting; make sure to have an instant-read thermometer available.)

5. Remove foil during last 30 minutes of roasting to brown top, if necessary. Cook turkey until juices run clear and internal temperature reaches 160° in thickest part of thigh, making sure thermometer doesn't touch bone. Transfer turkey to platter or carving board; loosely cover with foil and reserve excess juices for gravy. (Internal temperature will rise about 10° upon standing.)

6. Meanwhile, remove rack from Dutch Cast Iron pot; with spoon, skim excess fat from drippings. Place roasting pan with drippings across 2 burners. With whisk, stir flour into drippings until well combined; add remaining 2 cans broth. Heat 4 to 5 minutes over medium heat, stirring frequently to scrape brown bits from bottom of pan. Reduce heat

to medium-low; simmer 10 to 12 minutes longer or until gravy thickens, stirring occasionally. For smoother gravy, strain through fine-mesh strainer, if desired. Stir in remaining 1 tablespoon sage and 2 tablespoons lemon juice. Carve turkey and serve with gravy.

Tip: Plan ahead! When thawing a turkey in the refrigerator, it will take about 24 hours for every 4 to 5 pounds of turkey. Place the turkey in a container to prevent the juices from dripping on other foods.

To the readers: If you have a Dutch Cast Iron Pot—here is a great website I used for the first things I cooked in it: https://pinchofyum.com/10-easy-recipes-you-can-make-in-a-dutch-oven.

Dutch Cast Iron Pancakes
(this recipe came from Martha Stewart and is delicious!)

Ingredients

3 tablespoons unsalted butter, room temperature

3 large eggs

3/4 cup whole milk

1/2 cup all-purpose flour (spooned and leveled)

1/4 teaspoon salt

1/2 teaspoon pure vanilla extract

1/4 cup plus 1 tablespoon sugar

1 tablespoon fresh lemon juice

Recipe Preparation

1. Preheat oven to 425 degrees. In a medium cast-iron or ovenproof nonstick skillet, melt 2 tablespoons butter over medium heat; set aside.

2. In a blender, combine eggs, milk, flour, salt, vanilla, and 1/4 cup sugar. Blend until foamy, about 1 minute. Pour batter into skillet; bake until pancake is puffed and lightly browned, about 20 minutes.

3. Working quickly, dot pancake with 1 tablespoon butter, and sprinkle with 1 tablespoon sugar and lemon juice. Slice into wedges, and serve immediately.

Exciting News!

A percentage of all purchases of *Turkey Basted to Death* will be donated to the following two organizations!
Thank you for helping those that live with MS and homeless youth! For more information about those navigating life with MS, please visit https://www.nationalmssociety.org/ For more information about homeless teens, please visit https://truecolorsunited.org/

Read on for a sneak peek of *Blueberry Cobbler Blackmail,* coming February 28, 2020!

Chapter One

March 1, 2020

Dear Tabitha,

I'm sorry I was a no-show to our therapy session. Everything was closing in around me. Ava had something develop with her father and needed to hightail it to Santo Domingo ASAP. We scurried to get enough help from our employees and my family to cover the shifts at work. My family is all too willing to do anything for me after the last several months of insanity.

We've been gone close to three weeks so far, and you would not believe the newest mayhem to take place while we've been gone. I'm realizing that, regardless of the outcome, life is a journey of ups and downs and twists and turns. I realize it's necessary for me to continue my course of therapy with you, and I'm hoping you will be willing to schedule some more appointments when I return.

I've realized after the numerous, life-threatening events that have taken place, I need to figure out what it is I want for my future and work to make that happen. While on—do I dare call it a vacation?I mean, it is paradise here on the island, but the events have been anything but–vacation, I've met someone new. It's been a breath of fresh air, in spite of dangerous events, to find someone who I don't have a past with and to have an opportunity to make a new connection without Meiser or Keith around. Well, unless you count Meiser's video calls, texts, phone calls, and postcards...but otherwise, I've felt a freedom from family and the men in my life like I've never experienced, and it's giving me a new outlook on life!

I'm looking forward to getting into it all when I return to Leavensport.

Sincerely,

Jolie Tucker

Blueberry Cobbler Blackmail

*Family bombshells, family catastrophes, blackmail, and a trip that could be deadly...*and the new year has only just begun! After a disastrous Thanksgiving, Jolie Tucker is beside herself and feeling the walls closing in around her. She feels like she needs to escape Leavensport before she loses her mind. She unexpectedly gets her wish when her best friend and co-owner of Cast Iron Creations, Ava Martinez, gets a terrifying email revealing that her papa, Thiago, is in danger in Santo Domingo. The girls are off on a dangerous adventure in new territory. Will they be able to save the day before danger finds them?

Welcome to Leaven–oh wait!—Santo Domingo, where DEATH takes a Delicious turn!

About the Author

Moving into her second decade working in education, Jodi Rath has decided to begin a life of crime in her The Cast Iron Skillet Mystery Series. Her passion for both mysteries and education led her to combine the two to create her own business, called MYS ED, where she splits her time between working as an adjunct for Ohio teachers and creating mischief in her fictional writing. She currently resides in a small, cozy village in Ohio with her husband and her nine cats.

Links so we can Stay Connected

Be sure to sign up for a monthly newsletter to get MORE of the Leavensport gang with free flash fiction, short stories, two-minute mysteries, cast-iron recipes, tips, and more. Subscribe to our monthly newsletter for a FREE Mystery A Month at http://eepurl.com/dIfXdb

Follow me on Facebook at https://www.facebook.com/authorjodirath

@jodirath is where you can find me on Twitter

www.jodirath.com

Upcoming Release Dates

Coming February 28, 2020, Blueberry Cobbler Blackmail

Coming May 29, 2020, Cast Iron Stake Through the Heart

Coming September 4, 2020, Deep Dish Pizza Disaster

Coming December 18, 2020, Yuletide Cast of the Iron Skillet

www.ingramcontent.com/pod-product-compliance
Lightning Source LLC
Chambersburg PA
CBHW021700110726
47902CB00007B/2002